Ed Pinley

Paranormal Investigator

by

Lester Rogers

Available in digital

ISBN 978-1-960903-75-4 (paperback)

ISBN 978-1-960903-76-1 (hardcover)

Publify Publishing

1412 W Ave B

Lampasas, TX 76550

PublifyPublishing@gmail.com

Table of Contents

Chapter 1

Never Think Twice

My name is Ed Pinley. Previously, I had been a gun-carrying private detective for hire. At one time, I was a high-rolling big shot, complete with a big mouth, a bad attitude, and a love for money big money, the kind that comes from bad people and bad things. Living the high life makes one stupid, and it caught up with me one night when I chose to do one last job for a guy I thought was a friend. As it turned out, he didn't need a favor; he needed a scapegoat, and I was it.

Now don't get me wrong, greed played a major role in my demise. I knew I was working for a well-connected drug dealer, and I chose to take my chances. The job was easy, and all I had to do was park the van in a designated underground parking lot, get into another vehicle, and drive away. Bruno, the guy I did this work for, was nice enough to allow me to trade my services in return for a gambling debt I had run up at his joint in Vegas. I finished the job, and we were square.

A week later, he asked if I could do him another favor. He held out a round-trip ticket to one of my favorite gambling spots and a large roll of Ben Franklins. The money smelled good, so I took the bait, hook, line, and sinker. I found out that living on Easy Street makes one careless and too trusting of people. I should have been more careful, because I was working with people who were out to screw anyone they could. My buddy Bruno, apparently, was no different. I just didn't see it. And there you have it an occasional favor for a questionable friend, a few dirty cops. Shake well and pour it out.

Eight years of my life were spent behind bars. Time helps a person really look at their life, and looking back on everything, I realized my life had been a blur of bad choices. I had to face the fact that I had a few problems to deal with. There was that unquenchable taste for gambling, which led to a lifestyle I could not afford. Booze and living in the fast lane had led me down the road of stupidity and face-first into the wall of ignorance. That day, I drove the van Bruno gave me into the underground parking lot. I immediately noticed the unmarked police car.

The two police detectives got out of their car and approached me, their guns drawn and aimed at my head. That didn't bother me. I was more worried about the nylon stockings they had pulled down to cover their faces; I knew that wasn't standard police gear. One of the cops held a gun on me while the other cop took a key out of his pocket and opened the van doors. They stood there, silent, just staring into the cargo area of the van. One of the detectives started to place a silencer on the end of his gun, when the other pointed toward the street. They both suddenly left, and two police squad cars showed up just seconds after. I was arrested on the spot for drug possession and trafficking.

No one believed me when I tried to tell them what had just happened. I told them about the other two detectives that were just there. I told them that I recognized who they were and that I could ID them. That didn't go over so well. Everyone left the interrogation room, except Officer Delmonico. He took a particular interest in what I had just said, and he planted his fist deep into my lower abdomen, sending me to the floor. As I lay there gasping for breath like a flesh-eating guppy out of salt water, he leaned over me and gave me some free advice.

"Pinley, you had better shut up, or you could end up like Bruno." He threw a newspaper down next to me. After my blurred vision cleared, I saw that the headline read *"Bruno Santiago death ruled a suicide."* I learned that Bruno had been found hanging from a rope in his penthouse last night. That was the last time I saw him alive. He might have double-crossed me, but he got the worst end of the stick. I shut my mouth and took the rap.

Eight years later, I'm starting over. I got out of the protection racket and started my own business Ed Pinley, Psychic Astrologer and Private Paranormal Investigator. I have an internet operation, with operators standing by to offer advice and read futures. Meanwhile, I investigate insurance fraud, cheating husbands, cheating wives, ghosts, aliens from space, and the paranormal. Sometimes people hire me to investigate strange noises in the attic or strange sightings. It's way better than serving warrants or subpoenas.

Anyway, some people refer to my practice as a bubblegum detective, because I'm unarmed. I don't carry a gun because a felon can't own a gun. The only thing I can use as a weapon now is my brain. Some people believe that puts me at a disadvantage.

When I was released from prison, I moved to another location in the city. It was far away from the people I had known before going into the joint. And this area supported alternative ideas like paranormal investigations. For instance, two doors down from my apartment, there is a palm reader and dog whisperer that offers twenty four-hour emergency service. The Church of the Third Eye is right across the street, and they hold psychic bingo every night, from 6:00 p.m. to 1:00 a.m. From 1:00 a.m. to 6:00 a.m., it becomes an internet hub for Ed Pinley, America's only twice-convicted preordained male psychic astrologer.

So, there you have it. I was deep in the city, where things could be forgotten, and new starts were possible. I still had one bad habit left though. For some reason, I never think twice. I always go with my first gut reaction. It can make life interesting and a bit hazardous.

Chapter 2

✦

The Meeting

It was Wednesday, November 5 of the year 2018. I remember the day well. I had just returned to my office to catch up on some muchneeded sleep. It was almost 2:00 a.m., and I had been on a stakeout, hoping to get some pictures that would pay off. I struck out no pictures, no money. As I walked up to my office building, I noticed a new black 2018 Tahoe with tinted windows parked out front. This was unusual considering I was living in the hood now. The apartment I was renting had been the only rent I could afford at the time, and the protection fee was low. I opened the front door of the building and started to walk up the fourteen steps to my newly rented apartment. At the top of the stairway stood two large men dressed in black three-piece suits.

"Can I help you gentlemen?" I asked.

"My name is Agent Henderson, and this is my partner, Agent Frost. We have some questions for you, Mr. Pinley."

"I'm paid up on the protection fees. I have my receipt right here, boys. Besides, how do you know I'm Mr. Pinley?" I held out my receipt and watched their faces for some reaction, a clue to their intentions. Obviously, they had no sense of humor, and something else was on their mind.

"You're Pinley, and for your information, you are uglier in person. We would like to know if you have been contacted by this woman lately." Agent Henderson held out a faded black-and-white photograph.

"Why?" I asked.

The other agent, Agent Frost, glared at me and finally spoke. "Have you seen this woman?"

I took a closer look at the photograph. I admired her facial features, and she had a mysterious aura about her. "No, I haven't seen the lady. Say, you want me to find her?"

"Nice try, Pinley. We don't need your help. If she shows up, call this number immediately. You got it?"

Agent Henderson shoved his card into my top pocket and smiled slightly. Then the two men walked past me, down the stairs and out the door. I watched them from the hallway window as they drove away. Their Tahoe didn't have any plates, so I couldn't run their numbers to ID them. I was pretty sure they weren't a couple of nice guys out promoting positive community police relations.

I made a pot of coffee and stared out the window. The attractive woman in that picture was hard to forget. There was something about her, something indefinable. My gut told me she was dangerous, but if she walked through that door right now, I wouldn't think twice.

There was a soft, delicate knock on my metal fireproof door.

Then there was a rapid series of hard knocks.

"Hold on, I'm coming." I opened the door slightly and looked out through the crack. Standing before me was the same beautiful woman from that picture. She was slender, with long auburn hair that swirled down around her high cheekbones. Her eyes were green, and the look on her face had the feel of cold steel. Standing at attention directly behind her was a stocky man who was slightly shorter.

I quickly opened the door and held out my hand and tried to introduce myself. "Ed Pinley, private detective and paranormal investigator."

I continued to hold my hand out for a few more uncomfortable seconds as she walked past me and sat down in my chair at my desk. The gentleman smiled as he walked past me and stood behind her.

"Have a seat, sir," I said, pulling out a chair.

"He never sits. He has always stood, ever since we started working together." She smiled.

"That was probably a couple hundred years ago," the short stocky man said, laughing.

"Oh my, how time flies. By the way, I didn't get your name, Miss...?" I asked.

"My name is not important, Mr. Pinley," the lady said.

"I disagree. It helps in identifying whom one is talking with." Her physical beauty had just been marred by her overwhelming innate desire to be dominating, difficult, and demanding.

"Explain the paranormal investigating angle you have going, Mr. Pinley," the lady demanded.

I looked at her and then said, "Explain the two apes who were just here. They had a rather nice picture of you, and they were asking if you had acquired my services."

"I suppose in your business, you chase little green men in double-knit spandex," she said.

"They're not little green men, and I never wear spandex. Now what am I getting into, and what do I call you? I'm fresh out of numbers right now," I replied.

"We need you to escort me to a political dinner party tomorrow night."

"Sounds like a blast and innocent enough. You do realize that if you're looking for protection, I'm not licensed to carry a gun anymore, and I'm not in the protection racket."

"First of all, you won't need a gun, Mr. Pinley. Second of all, you will be escorting Mrs. Yang," the lady said.

"Wait a minute. I feel like we're getting somewhere. So, your name is Mrs. Yang."

"I'll be Mrs. Yang," she replied.

"What do you mean? So is your name not Yang?"

"My name's not important, as I said before. Let me spell it out for you. I'm someone impersonating Mrs. Yang. We are there to receive some information. Richard will be our backup if there are any problems," the lady added.

I looked over at Richard. He was still smiling and standing in the same spot. "And the information you're receiving is for Mrs. Yang? How does she feel about you impersonating her?" I asked.

"She has asked me to impersonate her. It's complicated, but she feels that her life could be in jeopardy if she attends the party. Mrs. Yang has asked me and Richard to help her."

"So, you're an actress, and Richard is your hired gun. I get it! Why do you need me?"

"You are a prop, Mr. Pinley. You are Mrs. Yang's younger escort. She likes men like you half her age, almost attractive but rough around the edges. You will fit right in."

I wasn't sure if she was complimenting me or not, so I went for the next logical question. "And how are you going to impersonate an older Chinese woman? Everyone there will probably know her. You are tall, slender, and fair to look at. Not to mention, you don't look even a bit Asian."

"Don't worry, Mr. Pinley. I've done it before. After I secure the information I need, we will meet up with Richard about a mile down the road, on the beach."

"I'm still wondering about your two buddies who were here earlier. They smelled like government agents," I said.

"To be honest with you, Ed, we are not robbing the place or committing any crimes against the government."

"So, we're on a first-name basis now. What's yours?"

"As I was saying, I'm receiving some information from a diplomat. The guys who visited you do not want me to receive that information. That's why I'm going as Mrs. Yang, with her blessing. They will be there, watching, hoping I might show up looking like this." She pointed at her body.

"So, you're a nameless activist?"

"Yes, if you must label me. And to answer your question, they are agents of your world government," she said, smiling at me.

"*World government!*" There were alarms going off in my head, and my mind raced desperately, trying to come to a rational conclusion. "What time does this party start?" I asked. I smiled at her, trying to make eye contact.

Immediately, she turned away, reached into her pocket, and pulled out her sunglasses.

I thought, *It is after 2:00 a.m. Why the sunglasses?*

"Richard will pick you up at 5:00 p.m. Dress for the occasion, Mr. Pinley." She turned away and started to walk out.

"Hopefully casual office attire and worn-out Keds will suffice." She turned back and looked at me for a few uncomfortable seconds. "Mr. Pinley, Richard will accompany you to acquire your wardrobe of course, at no cost to you. Then he will drive us to the dinner party. You will

8

escort me into the party and then wait while I meet with my contact." She smiled with authority. "Should I expect trouble?" I asked.

"You may want to think twice about this, Mr. Pinley. If you decide not to accept the job, we will understand," the lady said, her smile slight but noticeable.

"The problem is, Miss Nameless Activist, I never think twice once my interest is aroused," I answered.

"I know. That's why we picked you." She looked at the card that had been placed in my pocket by Agent Henderson, and she pulled it out. "Agent Henderson will want you to call him. I suggest you do so and give him my regards."

"How can I give him your regards if I don't know your name?" "You're full of questions, aren't you, Mr. Pinley? I like that." The two turned and walked out of my office, leaving the door ajar.

She was right; lots of questions filled my head one in particular.

I wondered how much I was getting paid for this clown act. One thing was for certain: tomorrow would be a very interesting day.

The next day, I woke up at 11:30 a.m. and realized I had neglected to call Agent Henderson. I got up out of bed and looked out my window. It was like it always was. You had the local meth head aimlessly wandering around, talking out loud. Then there were the local gang members driving around, making their appearance. My main concern was that Agent Henderson was out there lurking about, possibly spying on me. I wondered if he had seen my two visitors the night before. I reached for my cell phone and called him.

There was no answer, so I hung up the phone and grabbed my gym bag, a fresh towel, and a change of clothes and headed for the door. As I opened the door, standing before me was none other than Agents Henderson and Frost.

"Good morning, gentlemen." I smiled at the same two agents who were at my door late last night. "Did you get any sleep, Henderson? You look awful," I said.

"Very funny. I see that you finally called. You're late, Pinley," Henderson said.

"Yeah, well, I meant to call you last night, but I fell asleep. It was late after all. So, I called as soon as I woke up. That woman in the picture and a friend did show up right after you guys left."

"We know," Henderson said, smiling, as he held up a small square box, about a half inch in size.

"We filmed them coming up the steps and entering your apartment," Agent Frost said.

"Isn't that invasion of privacy, Agent Frost?" I asked.

"You didn't follow your instructions, Pinley. I think that's hindering a federal investigation," Frost replied.

"Touché, Frost. What else do you want?" "What's the bag for?"

"Heading for the gym. You can sniff and search it if you want. You have my permission."

Agent Henderson looked at the gym bag and smiled. "I don't need your permission, Pinley. Now what is your part in this?"

"I'm supposed to escort an older Chinese woman named Mrs. Yang to some event tonight."

Henderson and his partner laughed.

"What? What did I say that's so funny?" I asked.

"Nothing, Pinley. Forget about it. You know, I took you for a loser. Now I know you are. You're not an escort. You're a decoy. I hope you got paid up front. We know who to look for. We got her and her friend on video," Agent Frost said.

"By the way, be careful. I hear that being an escort can be dangerous," Agent Henderson added.

The two men turned away and walked down the stairs and out the door. I walked over to the hallway window and watched them leave.

I grabbed the bus to the Sweat Hall, my gym. It's a great place. "Low-Key, Low Fee" that is their motto. After an easy and refreshing workout, I stopped at the club to check the music lineup for Friday night. It was close to 4:45 p.m. when I arrived back at my office.

I looked out the window. A white limousine pulled up to the front of the building across the street, taking up the entire no-parking zone. A tall Black man slowly got out. He was dressed in a chauffeur's outfit, wearing white gloves and a white chauffeur's cap. The gang's squad car slowly rolled by, eyeing the man up close. The man paid no attention to them as he walked across the street toward my building. A few minutes later, there was a knock at my door.

"Mr. Pinley, it's good to see you again," he said as he entered my office.

It had occurred to me that I had never seen this man before in my life, so I asked, "I'm sorry, but who are you?"

"It's me, Richard. We were here last night, me and Zandra, the tall brunette. She gets moody sometimes, as you could tell. I was the smaller stocky white guy with her," the man answered.

"And today you're a tall Black man! I can tell this is no Al Jolson show. You're the real thing, and the guy last night was the real thing. What is this, some kind of carnival act? Where are the lady and the guy from last night? I need to tell them about some visitors I had this morning," I said.

"You called the agents, and the agents showed up. Mr. Pinley, that is good news. That's why Zandra told you to call them. They will be looking for last night's characters, which they probably have on camera. But tonight I'm Black, Zandra's an old Chinese woman, and you're our decoy. Beautiful, is it not? Now, Ed, we should be off to the men's store. Custom fit, of course. You will need to look your part." The man opened my apartment door and held it for me.

"Wait a minute. You're not Richard—at least, not the Richard I met last night. He definitely is white, and you're definitely Black. I need to know what I'm getting into."

"Mr. Pinley, to be frank with you, I'm not what I appear to be. Neither is Zandra. We are both different than you are," the man said. "Okay, so are you guys some sort of terrorist group? You know, they always say that sort of stuff. They always claim to be different or that they are doing God's work, and then everything starts blowing up all over the place," I said.

"We are not terrorists. We are a peaceful group, Ed, dedicated to world peace. What we are doing here tonight is gathering information. That is all."

I wondered about his comment of being different from me and was about to ask him, when there was a short burst of a police siren outside. I looked out the window. There was a police squad with lights on taking an interest in the illegally parked limousine.

"I hope you've got a legit license, Sunshine, because Officer Franklin has been known to be hard on some people, if you know what I mean," I said. I could see that the tall Black man claiming to be Richard had become nervous; the man's face began to bead up with sweat.

"Ed, that would be very bad," he said. He seemed to be struggling with how to say what he needed to say.

"It's all right. I know him," I said. "He'll just want to see your driver's license."

"Wait, Ed. There may be a problem with a license."

"In that case, you probably will end up changing clothes, from chauffeur duds right into a county-issued orange jumpsuit."

"Ed, I am a shapeshifter. I'm not as I appear." Before my eyes, he transformed back into his real shape. His skin was made of scales, large red-and-yellow scales. They moved like they were each breathing individually. He looked like a ten-foot-tall reptilian with human similarities. I was taken aback by the sight of it.

"I never believed in shapeshifting," I finally managed to say. "Ed, I am very real," the man said.

A second short siren blast came from the police squad outside.

"Ed, you've got to do something here. Everything depends on you." The man's eyes were big as he talked. Before my eyes, he shapeshifted back into the Afro-American person he had resembled and then into the white man I met the night before.

I still hadn't recovered from what I had just seen, when I went into survival mode. "Come on," I said. I got up and walked out the door. Richard was right behind me. "I'll do the talking, okay? You just go along with me."

We walked out the front door toward the double-parked squad. The cop was busy writing what looked like a short novel in his ticket book.

"Hello, Officer Franklin." I held my hand out toward Mark Franklin. He was once a friend from the police academy.

"Pinley, is that you? Ed Pinley! Imagine that. How are you anyway?" Officer Franklin asked.

"Not bad. Going on my first job since, you know, I recently got out."

"Yeah, I heard about that. You got the shaft, Ed. Everyone knows it. I heard your commercial on the radio. So you're a fortune-teller now?" he asked.

"I just hire the psychics and give them an honest wage for their work," I said.

"It's good to hear that, Ed."

13

"This is Richard. He's my driver. I'm escorting Mrs. Yang to an event out on Ocean Boulevard. Mark, it's my fault about the parking. I meant to be down faster. As it is, we are running very late."

"You're a male escort too? What's a male escort do these days anyway?"

"Not the way you think of it, Mark. Just a little security gig," I said.

"You do need a break, don't you? All right, get out of here."

Officer Franklin smiled as he talked. He winked at me as he drove off.

"Richard, those were scales I saw, and I refuse to wonder what Zandra looks like," I said when we were alone.

"Now you know, Ed. We are both shape-shifters. Zandra is a completely different species than me, but we still work well together," Richard replied.

I was hearing things that sounded unbelievable. Yeah, I'm supposed to be a paranormal investigator, and I am. But you don't have to believe in the unbelievable to investigate the unbelievable. Most of the time, you're just chasing somebody's imagination instead of an actual ghost.

Richard opened the back door of the limo, and I got in. I sat there thinking about everything I just saw and heard—the colorful breathing scales, world government agents, and a beautiful woman who was not a woman at all! Come to think of it, she was a totally different reptilian species. The thought of Zandra covered in scales, feathers, or what have you terrified my imagination. I was more out of control in this situation than I had ever been. I leaned forward and asked Richard a very important question, one I should have asked a long time ago.

"Be square with me. Is this all for real? Any minute, I expect William Shatner and a reality TV camera crew to show up," I said.

"Completely real and legal. We can't break the law. We have restrictions, like no violence. But we can passively interfere with things

14

or people. That's all we do. Tonight, Zandra will learn the location of an event we have interest in. And to be honest, you are the decoy. Believe me, Ed, there's nothing illegal about being a decoy or an escort," Richard said.

"What does it pay? I never asked you guys that either." "Probably not enough, boss!" Richard said in his butler voice (from the *Jack Benny Program*).

"Very funny," I said.

The limo came to a stop. The name on the glass door before us read "Geno's." It looked like a secret prohibition era liquor store from the Roaring Twenties. Richard opened my door, and I got out.

"You'll love this place, Ed." Richard opened the glass door to this windowless building. We walked in and saw an older man snoring loudly, his head resting on his desk. I began to laugh, and Richard signaled me to be quiet. We slipped by the sleeping clerk and entered a huge warehouse that was completely empty except for a box that was wrapped with twine. It was labeled "Ed Pinley." Richard picked up the box and smiled.

"We're all set, Ed. You're going to love how you look in this suit," he said.

"What? Are we doing commercials now? How do we know it will fit? I was never measured."

"Zandra sent your image to the tailor. It will fit." He motioned for me to follow him. We walked out, past the sleeping clerk and to our limo.

"Ed, you can change at Zandra's apartment," Richard said. "What about shoes?" I asked.

"It's all in there."

We drove toward the suburbs and finally came to a stop at the Alpine Condos, Building C. We got out, and I followed Richard into the building. He went to the first door and opened it. The place was empty—no furniture, no sign of inhabitance by anyone.

"Where's Zandra?" I asked.

"She'll be here momentarily. You had better change, Mr. Pinley." He led me toward a room in the back. There was a master bathroom, completely furnished. I showered and changed into my suit, equipped with shiny pointed shoes.

"She's going to love the way you look in that outfit," Richard said.

An old Chinese woman walked in and glanced over at Richard and me. "Are you ready, Mr. Pinley?" she said in Zandra's voice. "Zandra," I said.

"I see Richard revealed my name. I suppose he filled you in about us," Zandra replied, using her own voice.

"Yeah, I'm not sure I believe it yet," I said.

"You did say you were a paranormal investigator, Mr. Pinley.

How do I look? Real enough?" she asked.

"Very real. You look like a seventy-year-old Chinese woman." "I am a seventy-year-old Chinese woman. I am Mrs. Yang, the mother of a high-ranking Chinese official. And that high-ranking Chinese official has the information we need."

"What do I do then once I escort you inside?"

"Mr. Pinley, you will wait a short time while I see my contact. Then I will ask you to walk me to the powder room. On the way to the powder room, we will slip out the kitchen door in the back, head down the beach, and meet up with Richard. Is that easy enough, Mr. Pinley?" she asked.

"Let's go. We don't want to miss our opportunity," Richard said. The three of us left the apartment, Zandra as the old Chinese woman, me as her escort, and Richard as our chauffeur. We proceeded to the dinner party.

Richard performed flawlessly as the chauffeur, and I held my arm out for the elderly Mrs. Yang as I escorted her into the mansion on the beach. The place was enormous, with a lot of security. They looked like CIA, but I couldn't be sure. We made our way in, and another escort took over. I was led off into an adjoining waiting room.

From there, I could see the whole event taking place. Very important people were talking to other very important people while getting absolutely nothing accomplished. It reminded me of our senators and congressmen. Off in the background, lurking around, were Agents Frost and Henderson. They were awkward-looking and were obviously looking for Zandra and Richard. It occurred to me that Zandra was right about these two. They were looking for the beautiful young woman they had seen on video.

I watched as Mrs. Yang moved around the room, greeting people and talking with them. She slowly made her way to a Chinese man in his late fifties. They greeted each other, and I realized that this was Zandra's contact. Their meeting seemed painfully formal and short. They parted, and Mrs. Yang made her way toward me.

I stood as she approached. She grabbed my arm, and we walked down the hall toward the powder room, turning left into the kitchen just before we reached the powder room door. We made our way toward the back of the kitchen. We stopped when we saw that there were two security men outside the back door. Mrs. Yang backed up behind me and stepped around the corner as I counted our options and quickly realized there were none.

"All right, Ed, pick up that leash and take me out to go potty."

I turned toward the sound of Zandra's voice and saw a small ugly dog staring up at me with one good eye.

"Come on, we've only got a couple minutes left. Put the leash on me and take me out past these security guys. Tell them I have to go poo," the dog said in Zandra's voice.

Now you probably understand my dilemma here. Granted, I indulged in some minor drug activity as a very young adult. I never took anything stronger than mushrooms, and all that did was make me laugh uncontrollably and drink more beer. The small ugly dog was talking to me in Zandra's voice. Moments earlier, there had been an older Chinese woman with me, and now there was a small ugly dog with one good eye talking to me in Zandra's voice. My brain had frozen up.

"Come on, Ed. Snap out of it. We need to leave now," the small ugly dog said in Zandra's voice.

"Yes, ma'am. I mean…yes."

I put the leash on the small ugly dog, and we approached the door. The two security guys were immediately all over us.

"Sorry, no one goes out this way."

The small ugly dog began to whine, bark, and walk in circles. "We're not leaving. We're just going, you know, poo," I said. "No one leaves through this door. I have my orders," the security guard said. The security guard looked at me and then down at the small ugly dog as it walked in circles.

"She's ready now, boys. When she walks in circles, it's only a matter of time before she drops one," I added. The small ugly dog barked and wagged her tail.

"What do you think, Shawn? Do we let the dog go poo?" the security guard said, mocking me.

"I have never seen this guy before, but I do recognize the ugly dog," the other security agent said. The small ugly dog barked.

"I'm just doing Mrs. Yang a favor, but if it's a problem, don't worry about it. We are leaving in an hour. Maybe the dog can wait that long. See ya, guys." I started to turn and walk away.

"Okay, take the dog out. Just be quick. Stay where I can see you." The security guard opened the door, and the small ugly dog and I made our way out toward the shadows and the ocean.

A moment later, I heard the fire alarm go off. The two security guards began talking into their collar microphones, turning toward the door we had just come from. It sounded like all hell was breaking loose inside the beach house.

"Come on, Ed, run! Follow me!" The small ugly dog took off running, the leash dragging behind it.

I followed the dog, running as fast as I could. We had made it a few hundred feet down the beach when I stopped and looked back. Agent Henderson and his partner were coming out of the main entrance with their guns drawn. There was a crowd forming in the driveway. The agents made a quick sweep and then turned their attention to us.

"Hey, stop!" I heard Henderson shout.

I turned and started running again along the beach. I could see the small ugly dog just ahead of me. A moment later, I felt the impact of a slug entering my left shoulder. I spun around and finally came to rest face-first in the wet sand. I heard someone running toward me. I felt the impact of a concussion bomb, and I was blinded by the flash. I thought that at any minute, one of the government agents would finish me off with a bullet to the head. I felt someone pick me up and sling me over their shoulder.

"Hang on, Ed. We are going into the water." It was Richard; he was carrying me into the waves.

We kept going until we were swimming. The waves became bigger as we swam further out to sea. There were shouts and gunfire coming from the shore. Then there were searchlights in the sky and helicopters heading toward us. I began to panic, and I had trouble staying afloat. Richard grabbed me and wrapped his arms around my torso, and together we descended into a column of bubbles. I was in a panic.

"Ed, you can breathe."

I looked at Richard, amazed that I could hear his voice. "Go ahead and breathe, Ed," he said.

I took a breath. I was underwater, but I could breathe. Everything seemed to slow down; it became warmer all around me. I looked up and saw the lights skimming the water above us. We continued to descend deeper down the column of bubbles as the lights became smaller and smaller. I wondered what happened to Zandra after she had shape-shifted into that dog. I never saw what happened to her after I was shot. Richard was here, but there was no dog, no sign of Zandra. I wanted to ask him about her, but I couldn't speak. Things became blurry, and I felt like I had become frozen in time. As we descended deeper into the abyss, everything became pitch-black. I wasn't aware of anything—temperature, wetness, or sound. I was comfortable, very comfortable.

Chapter 3

Project Disarm

I opened my eyes. They slowly adjusted to the bright starlit night. I could smell the sea. I was floating on a small raft just offshore. I could feel the waves as the raft slowly made its way toward land. I remembered being shot. I felt my shoulder, and it was fine; there was nothing wrong. There was no gunshot wound, no blood. I looked closer at myself and realized I was in a US Air Force flight suit. The name Anthony Jibes was embroidered above the utility pocket.

It was then that I started to remember things, like landing facefirst on the sand, waiting to be shot in the head by Agent Henderson. There had been some concussion blasts. Then Richard had picked me up, and we made our way into the ocean.

Then I remembered other images and sounds. I was being carried into a brightly lit room. There was a sound, maybe a buzzing type of sound. There were four, maybe five oddly shaped forms standing around me. They placed me on a floating platform made of light. I was cold and could not move. One of the forms held a blue ball just inches above me. I could see lights shooting out of it and then entering my shoulder. I watched them for some time. Then slowly it became dark again, and I was floating again in midair. In the distance, I heard a familiar voice.

"Ed, can you hear me? You can wake up now," Zandra said.

I tried to open my eyes, but I couldn't. I could hear more coaxing from another voice. It was Richard.

"Ed, my man, can you open your eyes? Open your eyes if you can hear me," he said.

I opened one eye and saw two blurry figures standing beside my bed. Then slowly, the other eyelid lifted up to reveal a tremendously distorted group of figures standing before me.

"Ed, it will take a little time before you will be able to focus. The anesthesia they used affects the vision for a brief time," Zandra said.

"Where am I?"

"You are about three miles deep off the coast of Bermuda. Our people picked us up and transported us here. You had surgery three days ago." It was Zandra's voice I was hearing, but I still couldn't make out their images clearly.

"We have another assignment for you, Mr. Pinley, if you are up to it. You are in accelerated healing now, and in one week, you'll be better than new," she said.

Then it all came back to me the reason I was floating out here on this raft. What I was going to do sounded like a suicide mission, but Zandra had assured me that I would be all right. She said I was a great escort, but now they needed a Trojan horse and I was it. The facts are, I'm a sucker for a pretty woman, and she was not even the same species as me. Beautiful women have always gotten me into trouble, and I had a feeling trouble was coming soon. Then I remembered Richard filling me in on the details.

"Ed, we are going to put you on a raft just offshore. You will be put into an induced sleep mode to simulate fatigue while you float toward the beach. There is a small group of men guarding some stolen nuclear missiles. They will want to capture you," he said.

"So this is what you really recruited me for a suicide mission, so you can steal the missiles," I replied.

22

"No, Ed. We recruited you to get us into the camp. They will want to interrogate you as soon as possible."

"Trevor Wellington always uses the same interrogation team. They were in black ops together. We already have the interrogation team isolated. Richard and I will impersonate them. Once we arrive, Trevor Wellington will want to start the interrogation immediately.

Our hope is that we can isolate Wellington long enough for Richard to disarm the warheads," Zandra said.

"You mean, we don't have a plan for that?"

"You can't plan for everything, but one thing is for sure: there will be opportunity. We just need to seize it when it presents itself," Richard said.

"Who is this ex black ops guy?" I asked.

"Bad news. Trevor Wellington turned international arms dealer last year. He has lots of connections worldwide. The men with him are ex-military special forces. All of them, including Wellington, are wanted by the United States. Tonight, he is meeting with an unknown client to sell a few armed nuclear missiles ten, to be exact," Richard added.

"We arranged for an alert to go out worldwide with the US Air Force that one of their jets is missing two hundred miles southwest of Wellington's location. The pilot ejected before crashing. Wellington will assume that you are that downed pilot, and he will want to be sure you are that pilot." Zandra smiled.

"Wellington will want to interrogate you before his meeting, giving us just enough time to neutralize the warheads without anyone knowing about it," Richard added.

"What do I tell them? I've never been in the military," I said. "While you were in our hospital, we took the liberty of altering your looks. You now look younger, and we outfitted you with some implants. The implants will take over in these situations where your role is important to the mission," Richard replied.

"What do you mean by 'take over'?"

"You, the real you, will be disengaged while Anthony Jibes, US Air Force fighter pilot, will take over if Wellington interrogates you before we can arrive," Zandra answered.

"Once we arrive, as the interrogation team, we will ask Wellington to move us all to a private room," Richard said.

"When we are alone, I'll temporarily disable Wellington. Then you and Richard will go to work on the missiles," Zandra said.

"You want me to paddle to shore and give myself up?"

"Yes, but don't worry, they won't hurt or kill you right away.

They will want to interrogate you first." Richard smiled. "You mean torture."

"Don't worry, we will be there ASAP," Zandra added. "What about our exit plan?" I asked.

"Still working on that. There are a couple problems in transportation, but hopefully, we won't have to take the bus again," Zandra said.

I remembered our conversation just as it had happened a few hours earlier. And then my stroll down memory lane was cut short by blinding searchlights and threatening gestures by a small group of well-armed men. I held my hands up and surrendered.

I was taken to a small stone building and placed in a cell. There was a blanket on the floor and enough room to lie down. I waited for a visit from someone in charge. During that time, I fell asleep.

A short time later, I found myself standing in front of the man named Trevor Wellington. I was being held up by two soldiers, and Wellington was throwing water on me. I was trying to catch my breath. Apparently, they had been interrogating me, and I had passed out. I couldn't remember the beating I took, but I could definitely feel it now. There was a sound off in the distance; it sounded like a helicopter. I hoped it was Zandra and Richard masquerading as the interrogation team.

Wellington had his men carry me back to my cell. I listened to the sounds coming from outside my stone cell. There were three voices. One was Trevor Wellington's; the other two were male voices. They talked for a few moments, then the cell door opened. The guards grabbed me and put a blindfold on me. The three of us walked straight ahead. I heard a large door open and close behind me. They sat me down on a steel chair and handcuffed me to it. I heard Wellington talking to one of the two men.

"I want any information you discover fast, major," Wellington said.

"Yes, sir. All we need is a few hours. Liston is mixing the cocktail now."

Moments later, the blindfold came off me. All three men stood in front of me. One of the three placed his hand on Wellington's arm. A few seconds later, Trevor Wellington collapsed. They carried him over to the chair and placed him in it.

"Hello, Ed. Sorry, we encountered bad weather, or we would have been here earlier," Zandra said.

I looked up and saw that she had shape-shifted back to her human form right in front of me, but I never really saw anything.

"I'm sorry for the pain you endured," she added. "I'm sure it will all be worth it."

I looked at her, and she smiled. It was funny, but that smile made me feel like a million bucks. I would probably do it all over again if she asked me to.

"What did you mean about taking the bus?" I asked.

"I thought you'd ask that. It simply means that our planning and calculations had been incorrect, and we will have to create an innovative way to complete our mission and live through it," she replied.

"Oh. Nice."

"How are you feeling?" She looked at my face.

"A little sore, but I'll be all right. It's strange. I don't really remember the beating I took," I said.

"That was the implant taking over. That way, you could never accidentally give up any information under duress," she said.

"Implants. Just how many did you guys put in me anyhow?" "As many as needed. There is one helping you with the pain

from the physical trauma you have endured." "What happened to Wellington?" I asked.

"I squeezed his arm, and it was night-night time," she said, smiling. She showed me her ring. On the bottom side, it had a short needle sticking out.

Richard had shape-shifted back into his human form as well. He uncuffed me, and we walked back into the building. I saw the missiles mounted on a Chinese military truck. Richard handed me an array of special tools wrapped up in a leather case. I followed him over to the missiles. We started taking off the outer plate. It was amazing; I knew exactly what to do. I assisted Richard, and we mounted a small black chip into each missile head. Three hours had passed by the time we finished with the warheads.

Wellington sat at the table. He looked like he was in a trance. "Ed, we need to take our original positions. I need to handcuff you to the chair. Zandra and I will shape-shift into the two interrogators. The drug Zandra gave Wellington not only knocked him unconscious, but it will also be a memory inducer when he wakes up. All we need to do is suggest a memory, and he has that memory. He will not be aware of the lost time. All he will see is me giving you this injection," Richard said.

"You will begin showing signs of having a reaction to the drug. Richard and I will know what to say," Zandra said.

I saw Richard spray something into Wellington's nostrils. He opened his eyes. Before I knew it, they plunged a needle into my arm. I watched as Major Liston injected me. The noise all around me became louder; I could feel it. My vision was crystal clear. I realized then that I was hovering above everyone, floating in midair, looking down on everyone and my body. I watched the three of them as they discussed my condition. I saw my body thrusting about in violent convulsions.

"General, he is having convulsions just like before, sir," Major Liston said.

"I see that," Wellington replied.

"This seizure is worse than the last four. Thank you for your assistance, sir," Major Shoemaker said.

I watched as my body stopped shaking violently. I lay there, still foaming at the mouth.

"It is almost time, according to my watch. We've been at this over three hours," Wellington said.

"Yes, sir. You requested that we be thorough," Shoemaker said. "I know."

"No pulse," Liston said.

"That is confirmed, sir," Shoemaker added.

"Don't bring him back again, and get rid of the body. Stay out of sight until we make the exchange. There's a room in the back.

Stay there till I come back. I don't want to spook these people," Wellington said.

"Yes, sir," Liston replied.

I watched as Wellington went out the metal door. Zandra and Richard walked over to the chair I was handcuffed to. My body lay still. They uncuffed me and placed my body on a gurney. Then they wheeled my body out through the back door. It opened up to a landing pad for a helicopter. I could see everything from my position. I hovered above them as they talked.

"Richard, are we safe here?" Zandra asked.

"Yes, I have a clear view of the area. I'm collecting data right now. As we speak, I can see the truck carrying the missiles. Wellington and his men are positioned north of the truck," Richard said.

"Okay, let's bring Ed back." Zandra sprayed something into my nostrils.

I watched as Richard lifted my body up to a sitting position. I saw my one eye open for just a split second, and then I was suddenly conscious, looking at the two of them.

"What did you do to me?" I asked.

"Relax, Ed. You made it. You just had a near-death experience.

How do you feel?" Zandra asked.

"Great actually, considering I was having convulsions." I wiped off some of the dried foam around my mouth.

"The exchange is about to happen. Richard is recording everything that takes place, as evidence," she said.

"Where is the camera?"

"He records all the data through his eyes. It is sent directly to our command post and stored, in case we don't make it out of here alive." Zandra laughed.

Somehow I knew she was going to say that. I didn't care though; it was a great evening. I had my first near-death experience, and I felt great. I was looking forward to discovering who the buyers were. I looked out toward the ocean. The waves were smaller now. The sun had nearly gone down, and it seemed quiet and peaceful. I noticed a spot in the ocean that seemed illuminated. It became brighter as I watched it.

"Richard, Zandra, do you guys see that?" I asked. I pointed out toward the ocean. The ocean was bubbling up with tremendous force. The light was transparent, lighting up the entire area. We watched as the large transparent oval-shaped object rose up and hovered above the water. From our viewpoint, it looked to be as big as a cruise ship. It began to make its way toward shore. Wellington and his men watched as the vessel made its way to them. I could see that he had a few shooters in place for insurance. He had four marksmen covering the exchange.

We watched as the vessel made its way toward shore. It made no sound as it approached the area where Wellington and his men were waiting.

"We have confirmed that the vessel is a Rufilian warship. Wellington is the arms supplier. Once we witness the exchange, we can make our way out of here," Richard said.

"Who are the Rufilian?" I asked.

"The Rufilian are an ancient enemy of ours. In our own dimension, the Rufilian conquered the human race on the surface. During that fifty-year war, they slaughtered billions of people. They took all the young women and children for their breeding stock. They executed every male, starting at age twelve, and kept a few for breeding," Zandra said.

"Didn't you know of the wars on the surface?"

"Yes, but we kept to ourselves, thinking the Rufilian would stop after they had conquered the surface. The humans were as violent as the Rufilian were. My ancestors were a peaceful reptilian species, smaller, with passive defensive capabilities, like shape-shifting. We kept to ourselves, away from the humans and away from the Rufilian."

I looked at Zandra. She had sadness written all over her face something I wasn't prepared for.

"When the Rufilian finally conquered our defenses, they used the remaining survivors as breeding stock. It was that breeding program that created all the survivors here today. Richard, myself, and everyone on our warship are the products of that breeding program, half human and half reptilian. They were trying to gain some of our traits, like shape-shifting," she said.

"It sounds like they were trying to create the perfect worker race."

"The half-breeds, like myself and Richard, we were bred for service, especially for the military. It was hard times. We did things I regret." Zandra turned away from me and watched the exchange that was about to take place. There was an awkward silence before she spoke again. "Something the Rufilian did not take into consideration was the aggressive genes they gave us. After almost fifty years of slavery, the half-breeds declared war on the Rufilian. There was an uprising. The half-breeds took to the street. They were outgunned, but they held on. Then they made their way to the Rufilian command center. It was suicide, but they still tried."

"Why did they attack the command center?" I asked.

"The Rufilian had developed technology that could open a portal to another dimension. It had never been tried with live specimens. No one knew if it would work. The Rufilian were going to test it on the insurgents, and the insurgents knew that. The insurgents took the command center and gained access to the device. Once the insurgents started the procedure, the energy grid was tapped. The portal opened. Our group of insurgents rushed toward the wall of blue mist. They were successful in using it to transport the remaining survivors of our race to your dimension. The war party that was in pursuit of the insurgents had also been transmitted to your dimension," Zandra said.

"That would be the Rufilian we see here now," I said.

"That is a problem the secret world government is trying to deal with, trying to track down and capture the Rufilian before they detonate a nuclear bomb, causing an unstoppable world war. Opus 8 is a secret worldwide task force. They're an international black ops team consisting of Western and Eastern governments and their allies.

Henderson and Frost are part of that team. Their mission is to track the Rufilian activity and intervene wherever possible. Basically, the secret world government has secretly been at war with the Rufilian ever since the Rufilian killed President Lincoln."

"They killed President Lincoln!" I said.

"Yes, and a few others. Soon after that, a world government was secretly formed. And since then, the established world government calls all the shots worldwide. Your president and congresses are for show, just like the Queen of England, Parliament, and all the other pompous world leaders. The world government is in charge and in competition with the Rufilian for dominance over the whole earth. But there is good news though!" Zandra exclaimed.

"What is that?" I asked.

"We have disarmed the missiles, and now we can track the weapons. We can rest assured knowing the missiles will not ever detonate. When they do try to launch, we will pinpoint their exact location and swoop down on them before they know it."

We both looked over at the hovering vessel. There was a wall of shimmering light almost two hundred feet tall reaching from the base of the vessel all the way to the ground. Two Rufilian soldiers walked out from behind the shimmering light. Their size was threatening; they towered over everyone by over five feet.

The Rufilian soldiers motioned for Wellington and his men to drive the truck carrying the missiles into the light. We watched as the truck disappeared into it. Then Wellington and his two bodyguards walked into it. A few moments later, the two bodyguards' bodies flew out. Their limp crumbled bodies lay on the ground. Moments later, the driver was tossed out of the light, and he lay motionless on the ground next to the guards. Immediately, the Rufilian soldiers began firing on Wellington's shooters before they could react. In a matter of a few seconds, all of Wellington's men lay dead, their bodies scattered on the ground like paper-mache dolls.

Without warning, the buildings all around us were fired on by the Rufilian warship's lasers. We all turned to run. I felt the heat and then the surge of flying debris. I was lifted off the ground and into the air. I landed hard; it felt like I was crumpled into a ball. I lay there unable to move.

It seemed like a long time passed before I realized I no longer had arms or legs. I tried to look around, but my face was covered in blood and my vision was blurred. I began to panic. Unable to move,

I wanted to die. Then I felt their presence. They were huge shapes; Rufilian soldiers were looking down at me. Again, I tried to move. I wanted to run; I wanted to fight back. But I couldn't.

They lifted me up and placed me on a stretcher. They strapped my head down using a strap across my forehead; I winched as a Rufilian tightened it up. Then they placed a strap across my bloody torso. Another Rufilian wiped my face clean of blood and picked out pieces of shrapnel. The other shapes were placing tubes in my torso, although I could not feel it.

They carried me away into a room. I saw the reflection of their oddly shaped hands in the large stainless-steel reflector mirrors on the surgery light. Then one of the huge figures began to shave the top of my head. I saw in the reflection a device that looked like a multiheaded drill in the hand of the huge shape. I tried to scream, but I couldn't; the huge hand gently pushed an oxygen mask down, covering my mouth. I waited for the pain of those drill bits ripping into my skull. Then the silence came. I lost consciousness.

Chapter 4

Lost Time

I woke up and listened to the sounds in the room before I completely opened my eyes. I opened them slowly, and as my eyes adjusted to the dark, I tried to remember...anything. But there was nothing no memory of where I was or how I got here. I looked around and realized I was in my apartment, lying on my bed. I hadn't been home since the mission with Zandra and Richard. According to my memory, it didn't go well. I looked at my arms and legs; they were there all right. I got up and turned on the light. I looked at myself in the mirror. I was in a one-piece bodysuit made out of strange fabric, but in my memory, I was in US Air Force attire. I started to undress to see if I had visible scars.

"Welcome back."

I looked over and saw Richard and Zandra standing at the door. "We thought you would never wake up," Richard said.

They both stood there, larger than life, smiling from ear to ear. Zandra was as stunning as ever, and Richard, the first-class gentleman, was still Mr. Positive himself. These were two of my favorite reptilian people in the world. I was speechless and a bit overcome with emotion.

"How are you feeling, Ed? You have been slowly waking up for the last few days," Zandra said.

"I feel great, not even stiff. How long have I been asleep?"

"It has been a few months, Ed. You have been in a medically induced coma. That's why you may not have any memory, except for maybe the last few minutes you were last conscious. The doctors have had you on an accelerated healing program, utilizing that bodysuit you are wearing. The suit exercised your body while you were recovering, keeping your muscles active.

"When the doctors decided to bring you back, we thought it would be best here, in your own place. We need to see how you do without the suit on. It may take a little time for you to get used to not having the suit assist you. You will need to start working out and slowly get back into shape. We will wait out here while you change, and then we can go to the gym you used to work out at."

I changed out of the suit. I could feel the difference; my legs and arms were weak in fact, I felt weak all over. I looked at my arms and legs. There were no scars, no appearance of skin grafting. I walked out into the kitchen, where Richard and Zandra were sitting.

"I remember being captured. They put me on some kind of stretcher, but I didn't have any arms or legs," I said.

"You were severely injured during that attack. We tried to reach you first, but the Rufilian beat us to you. We watched them take you away. We could see you were still alive. We watched as the Rufilian prepared you for life support. That's when we realized they were trying to save your life and were going to transport you," Richard said. "Normally, they would have killed you in front of everyone.

They would have tortured you, hoping to draw us out and have us attack them. We would have been forced to watch and take no action." Zandra hesitated for a moment, and then she smiled. "So we were excited that they took you. We knew you were alive, and that gave us time to find you."

There was a quiet moment. I looked around my apartment. It was just as I had left it. Actually, it looked in better shape than I had left it.

"I see I still have a place. What about my business?" I asked

A woman walked into the room. "I have taken care of everything as if I was you." She looked at me. She had dark-brown eyes that demanded all your attention. She smiled, and before my eyes, she turned into me, my exact replica. I was standing face-to-face with myself. It was apparent to me that this woman was a shape-shifter, like Zandra and Richard.

"You see, Mr. Pinley, while you were helping Zandra and Richard, I was here being you. I must say, that phone scheme is golden, Mr. Pinley. You are building up quite the bankroll," the woman said.

"And while you're not being me, who are you? What is your name?"

"Zandra said you were big on names," she replied. "My name is Violet. I am the younger sister of Zandra same father, different mothers. Would you like some coffee, Mr. Pinley?"

"Yes, I'd love some. I can't remember the last time I had coffee." I watched as she poured out coffee into mugs. "And by the way, you may call me Ed."

Violet smiled. "Do you remember anything after the Rufilian laser attack?" she asked.

"I don't have any recollection of events after I lost consciousness. I remember running from the lasers and being hit."

"Opus 8 and our special forces searched for the Rufilian for nearly two weeks after your capture. It was then that we finally got a break. The Rufilian fired all ten missiles at their targets," Richard said.

"We were able to sweep in and capture them before they realized the bombs hadn't detonated. The tracking devices you and Richard installed were successful," Zandra said.

"What about Wellington?" I asked.

"Wellington and you were being kept alive as part of an experiment," Richard replied.

"The Rufilian were trying to identify and capture a human soul as it leaves a deceased person's body. By the time we captured the Rufilian warship, Wellington had already died. Our research teams are still investigating the devices they had hooked up to him," Zandra said.

"They were hooking you up to that same device they had Wellington hooked up to, when Richard and Zandra captured the Rufilian warship you were being held in. The security forces captured the entire colony, 2,600 or more Rufilians," Violet added.

This woman was sharp. No surprise, seeing as how she was a sister of Zandra. I watched her as she poured the coffee. She was every bit as breathtaking as Zandra.

"You are a medical mystery, Ed. Our surgeons were able to attach the bionic arms and legs we had designed to your torso. We were able to grow and attach synthetic human skin to your existing skin using reptilian DNA," Zandra said proudly.

"Sounds like your people have a lot invested in me," I said. "Ed, you almost lost your life for us. We felt that trying to just keep you alive would be inhuman. You were a complete amputee," Violet said.

"You would have needed around-the-clock assistance feeding yourself, not to mention all the other necessities. You would have led a miserable existence. Instead, we took the chance that your new arms and legs would work. The bonus was that you were healthy. We never tried the skin transplant on a human before, but it worked," Zandra said.

"Finally, it was your tenacity and your will to live that pulled you through. We knew you could do it, Ed." Richard smiled.

"Mr. Pinley" Violet began. "Call me Ed," I said.

"There is some history you should know before we proceed. It will help you understand the situation better."

Everyone sat down as she talked.

"In our dimension, we were trying to escape from the Rufilian. Dranco was the Rufilian commander. He was a half-breed like Zandra and Richard, but the difference was, he was all reptilian, bred from two different reptilian species. Zandra and Richard were his enforcement team, handpicked by Dranco himself, even though they were half human."

"Richard and Zandra were your enemies at one time?" I asked. "Yes, they were. During the escape attempt, they switched sides. They saved a lot of lives and risked their own lives doing so." Violet smiled and then continued. "Our mission was to overrun the laboratory that had an experimental device that could open a portal to other dimensions. We wanted to escape through the portal into any dimension, with our warships and as many survivors as we could, in order to escape the Rufilian. Dranco, Zandra, and Richard followed us in hot pursuit. Zandra and Richard were on the ground, running toward the portal opening. Dranco was on the ground, running close behind them."

"I had the device in my hand. My orders from Dranco were to close the portal door before the rest of the survivors could escape. Instead, I threw the device away," Zandra said.

"More Rufilian warships approached and began firing on the remaining survivors making their way to the portal. It could have been a slaughter. I saw Zandra pull her weapon and begin firing on the approaching Rufilian warship, hitting it several times, causing it to crash," Violet said.

"Our warships and some of us had already passed through the portal. I heard Zandra tell Richard to go back for survivors and get as many through the portal as he could. Then I saw her take a hit. I saw her fold like a paper doll." Violet's voice cracked a bit as she spoke.

"Her body lay limp on the ground. Dranco reached her seconds later. I saw him pull his weapon out. I thought he was going to kill her, so I aimed my gun at him. He picked Zandra up and put her over his shoulder. He turned and fired several times on his own warship. The warship stuttered and started to descend out of control. Dranco ran toward the portal opening with Zandra on his shoulder. I saw that he had the box in his hand. He must have picked it up when he started to approach us. When I looked again, he and Zandra were gone," she said.

"It was chaos when we all landed here in your dimension. It was a new world. We all arrived in the same location. It was on the shoreline of the Northwest Pacific Ocean," Richard said.

"Richard and I began looking for Zandra and Dranco. Then off in the distance, I saw the Rufilian warship that made it through the portal. It was struggling to stay in flight. We watched as the warship attempted to crash-land on the ocean and then sank," Violet said.

"We looked everywhere along the beach. Still there was no sign of Zandra or Dranco, and we couldn't find the crashed Rufilian warship or any survivors," Richard said.

"Richard and I continued to searched the area, and we found Zandra. But there was no sign of Dranco," Violet said.

"I don't remember much after I was hit. I do remember being carried by Dranco and being laid down on the ground. He said that we were safe and that help was coming for me. I tried to ask him to stay, but he said that there were soldiers hunting for us, that he had to take them out or lead them away from there. He said goodbye and left. That was the last time I saw him," Zandra said.

There was uneasiness in the room. It felt like one of those meetings I used to attend when I worked for the mob. There were questions and hard answers.

"The sunken Rufilian warship must have survived the depths of the ocean, and the survivors rebuilt it. And now, as of today, all the Rufilian known to exist in our dimension have been captured, and Wellington is finished. That leaves Dranco. We have no signs, no proof of his existence. As far as we can tell, he disappeared after tending to Zandra. Some of my fellow soldiers say he went back through the portal, back to our dimension. But there are some clues that are worth looking at." Violet stopped and looked around the room.

"If one looks for cultural clues, like stories of strange events and monsters, stories of swamp monsters, legends, and especially Indian stories passed down through generations, there are hints of Dranco. I believe he was a friend to the Indians. There are many stories of a creature helping lost hunting parties caught in bad weather, leading them home. They called him a skin-walker because he would change into a fourteen-foot-tall bipedal reptile. That was his natural state, but the Indians didn't know that. He defended them against other predators and hostile tribes.

"He would often shape-shift into Hector Red Feather, a tribal elder known by everyone. The Indians thought that Hector Red Feather was his natural body. Dranco was the first to leave when white men started to settle in South Florida. The Indians say he headed for the swamps of the Louisiana Territory. I believe he is still there, alive and well. I think Ed and I should investigate. I've made some contact with some local experts in that area," she said.

"I like the idea," Zandra said.

"But first, Ed needs to get back into shape. That may take some time," Richard said.

We walked over to the gym. It was taxing. Once we were inside, I started slowly and kept at it.

It took almost a month before I felt I was back to my old self. Violet had been working on making contact with people who may have had contact with any swamp monster. She walked into the kitchen to grab some water.

"Have you decided where we're going?" I asked.

"We are going into the middle of some bayou in search of a swamp monster and ghost. There are lots of legends and some very fresh sightings of a creature that matches a bipedal reptile that turns into a man named Curtis, a local legend. Some locals believe that Curtis isn't a ghost, that he is still alive at the age of 122. They have stories of this old man appearing out of nowhere and helping distressed hunting

39

parties. Everyone who has seen this Curtis guy swears he is alive and in the flesh," Violet replied.

"There may be a problem with that plan, Violet," Richard said. He pointed a pen at the wall. A blue light appeared, then a screen.

The operations commander began to speak. "We have intelligence that the United States Homeland Security has quarantined the area known to us as Bleachers Wash, one hundred square miles of waterways and swamps."

"That's the area Curtis was recently seen at," Violet added. "Opus 8 is assisting in the operations as well. We received information that their black ops teams are in place. The Black Swann and her interrogation team were notified and were en route as of this morning. Our ops team intercepted her and her team. Zandra, Richard, Violet, and Ed, you will go as the Black Swann and her interrogation team. Be ready to leave as soon as possible. Travel arrangements are in place," the operations commander said. "Zandra, you will be briefed while your team gets ready. Richard, gather everything you need. Violet, prepare Mr. Pinley for his face mask."

The screen disappeared.

I looked at Violet. She had a case placed on the table. She reached into the case and lifted out a transparent hood. It was shaped from the top of the head to the neck, and it looked like a knight's headgear, with the braided steel mesh beads.

"This face mask can be programmed to highlight various traits, like high eyebrows, a large nose, a small nose, and your lips and cheekbones. In other words, you'll look different. It's a disguise that blends into your skin, completely undetected. I decided that I like you bald, with large eyes, small ears, and a crooked nose." Violet smiled.

"I like that you can make me into the man of your dreams from the neck up."

We both laughed. I felt good and very excited for an adventure.

Chapter 5

In Search of Curtis

I sat in the very back seat of our black SUV. Richard, as our driver Mr. Simms, expertly guided our bulletproof SUV toward a group of tents and trailers set up at the edge of the open water. Zandra, as the Black Swann, sat in the passenger seat. Violet was the team doctor, and I was her assistant. Zandra turned to face us in the back.

"Ed, you are the newest member to this team. The guy you're replacing was captured last year. These people know that, but with you being the newest recruit, there may be some questions by Opus 8 at first," she said.

"That will be the distraction we need to achieve our goal," Richard added.

"Great, that means they are going to torture me again, right?" I said.

"Everything you need to say will come naturally. Some of it may surprise you," Violet said, smiling at me.

"Yeah, but torture?"

"They won't torture you, but they may ask you for some details about your last job," Richard said.

"They want to make sure you are who you say you are," Zandra said.

"Of which I'm not," I added.

41

"By the time they figure that out, we will be well on our way," Richard replied.

Our car glided to a stop. Armed guards opened our doors as we got out. They pointed at me and motioned for me to go with them. Two guards marched me off as the Black Swann and her team walked toward a heavily guarded semitrailer. Outside, standing by himself, was a lone Opus 8 agent.

"Madam Swann, it's nice to see you under these unique circumstances," Agent Harris said, grinning.

"Yes, Agent Harris, very unique. Where have you taken my assistant?" the Black Swann asked.

"We want to ask him a few questions," he replied.

"You said there would be no arrests for past offenses against Opus 8 if we helped you," she said.

"Yes, but his testimony will help us in our efforts. It might make or break our inquiry."

"How long do we need to wait?" she asked.

"You will have to do it without him for now," Agent Harris said.

He led the group over to a large tent.

"What is it we must do? I've brought everything we need for a lethal interrogation. I can make it last a long time in order to extract as much information as possible. I can also use more conventional ways of extracting information if that is required. But I need my whole team."

Harris ignored Madam Swann as he answered his cell phone. "Harris." There was a long pause. "Okay." He placed his phone in his pocket. "Sorry, your assistant may not make it. I've been told he reacted negatively to some of the questions. They're trying to revive him now. Follow me, and you can view the prisoner," he said.

"Harris, if he dies, you may as well start counting your days right now," Madam Swann said.

"Don't threaten me on my turf. I can still have you all arrested right now," he said.

"I believed you when you said there would be no tricks," she said.

"This isn't a trick. Sorry about your guy."

"And did you get what you needed?" she asked. "No comment."

Agent Harris opened the door to the tent and walked into a dimly lit area. There was a large water tank on the floor. It was almost ten feet high and twelve feet long. Inside was something dark and large. It hardly moved.

"I can't make it out. Harris, is this display a joke?" Madam Swann asked.

"Have you ever heard of a shape-shifter? They can assume various shapes. Others call them skin-walkers," Harris said.

"Very funny, Harris."

"I'm not kidding. That thing in there was captured by my team. I have ten men who saw it shape-shift from a man into this thing. We caught it seconds after it shifted."

Harris turned on a light, which illuminated the tank. They observed the creature for about ten minutes.

"Not a lot of movement. It must be dead," Madam Swann said.

Outside, there was a large commotion, and then sirens. Harris looked at a message on his phone.

"Shit. I'll be right back. If anyone tries to leave this tent, you will be shot on sight. Understand?" he said as he left in a hurry.

The door closed. Richard looked at the object in the tank. "It is a Zeblaft from our dimension," he said.

"Harris said they saw it shape-shift into this," Madam Swann replied.

"They saw a man shape-shift into the shape of this creature while they managed to capture this thing. It's a decoy. Whatever this is, it is not alive. It never was," Richard said.

"What do you mean?" she asked.

"Oh boy, look at that. It also has an explosive device in it." "Is there a way to disarm it?" Violet asked.

"No, and it looks like we have ten minutes before it goes off. I can see the timer now."

"They never saw this?" Violet asked.

"I have the ability to see through layers. They must not have x-rayed this thing," Richard said.

"We can go through the back door of this tent, but they are armed. We won't make it far looking like this," Madam Swann said.

The door swung open, and Harris stormed in. "Your guy is holding my security team hostage. He demands to see you all, or he will start killing one every five minutes." He looked at the tank the creature was in.

"I thought my guy was dead, Harris." Madam Swann smiled. "Harris, this is not a skin-walker or shape-shifter," Violet said. "Actually, it's a bomb," Richard said.

"A bomb!" Harris exclaimed.

"Yes, and we have less than ten minutes before it detonates," Richard added.

"Swann, you know what this means?" Harris asked.

"Yeah, your ass, you have a lot to explain. You bring in a wanted terrorist group, allow them to take hostages, and capture a shapeshifter that turns out to be a bomb. Nice job, boss. Now let's get my guy, and we will safely leave here," Madam Swann said.

Harris walked out of the trailer with the Swann team. Across the way, standing on the dock by the open water, I stood with five men who were bound and gagged and on their knees.

"Looks like you pissed him off, Harris," Madam Swann said. "Are you guys all right?" I asked.

"Yes. Good job, by the way. Our friend Agent Harris has offered to let us all leave safely if we give him back his security team," Madam Swann said.

"These guys aren't very nice. Are you sure we shouldn't kill them all? After all, we are here now," I said.

"You're right, but I gave my word to Harris that there would be no tricks. Besides, the rest of their men will be back any minute. So I guess we should move on. I think we helped out here as much as we could. There is one thing we should consider. Everything is about to blow up."

"Yes, Madam Swann. I have a boat ready for boarding tied to the dock."

Madam Swann gagged and tied Harris up, leaving him with his security team on the dock. The Swann team untied the boat and headed for open water.

"Good job, Ed. I'm proud of you," Violet said, smiling.

"Everything went just as planned, Richard." Zandra had already shifted into her human form. Violet and Richard followed suit.

"Ed, I've deactivated the mask. You can peel it off now," Violet said. her.

"Good. I feel great." The mask peeled off easily. I handed it to "What happened?"

"They started out nice. They started to read something to me.

I looked up, and the lights went out. I don't know if they hit me or what. Sometime later, I opened my eyes. I was inside a body bag. I could hear the men talking. I knew they were in the same room as me. I waited for them to leave. When I heard the door close, I slowly cut myself out of the body bag. Once out, I was able to assess the situation. I knew there were only five security people, and they were all visible from my viewpoint. I also knew that you were all inside the tent with Harris. Everything that happened from that moment on seemed surreal, as if something else was in control. I did things I did not know I could do. I said things that surprised me, and I acted very different from myself," I said.

"I told you, Ed, that this would be a little strange, but you will get used to it. You have advanced technology inside you, as well as a bionic set of arms and legs."

"Are you back to being Ed now?" Richard laughed.

"You acted according to our plans. It gave us enough time to see what they had," Zandra said.

"Thankfully, it wasn't Dranco," Violet said.

Off in the distance behind us, the bomb exploded. "Hope Harris and his men are all right," I said.

"I assure you, they were untied just in time," Violet said. We maintained a steady speed, heading out toward open water. Behind us, three boats were gaining on us fast.

"It looks like the rest of Harris's men showed up," Zandra said. "Excellent. This should do it for Harris. I bet he's going to be speechless. Everyone, ready on three, and we'll be in the water. One,

two, three," Richard counted.

We all fell effortlessly over the side of the boat and into the ocean. We drifted downward, surrounded by bubbles as we descended into the deep. Above us, the speedboats raced toward our abandoned speeding boat. Again, I was at peace as I floated down toward our awaiting vessel. It was good to be alive.

Chapter 6

Curtis the Legend

It was nice to be home again. Violet was cooking Santiago Gank for Zandra, a mixture of mystery roadkill meat from a species indigenous to the Midwest and other unnamed additives. Richard had been sleeping in my bed for nearly two days now. Zandra was bathing; it had been almost ten hours since she had entered the bathroom. Nevertheless, I was glad to be home in one piece.

When Zandra walked in, her nostrils flared up. "Smells good," she said.

It was then that my nose discovered the rancid smell of Santiago Gank. The smell gagged me; tears ran down my face as I helplessly dry heaved while on my knees.

"Try running the water. That's what I do." Violet walked over and turned on the water.

Zandra took the plate of food and sat in the other room. "What's wrong with Ed?" she asked as she sat down at the table.

"Food reaction," Violet replied.

"Oh, that happened to you once, didn't it?" Zandra asked. "Yes, the first time I made Santiago Gank." Violet laughed.

Meanwhile, I nearly dry heaved to death. I somehow made it outside. How I managed to get down the steps, I don't know. My vision was blurred from the tears.

"Mr. Pinley." It was the delivery guy. "Are you all right?" "I'm okay. Just a little bad air. Thanks," I said.

"Timing is everything. I have a letter for you, Mr. Pinley. Sign here to confirm that I hand-delivered it," the delivery guy said.

I signed the receipt and took the letter. "Thank you." He bicycled off.

I looked at the postmark. It was from Gauthier Parish, Louisiana, addressed to me, Ed Pinley Investigations. I decided to get some strong coffee before I returned to my apartment. I made my way to Louie's Coffee Cart and then proceeded to my apartment.

"I have a letter here, hand-delivered."

Violet picked it up and looked at it. "It's from the outfitter I was in contact with. He used the private secure delivery service we offered on one of our pamphlets," she said.

She opened up the letter. The printed letterhead read "Crazy Willie, Bayou Guide and Outfitter." Scribbled in was the sentence *"The government has come, just as you said they would. What you are searching for has found sanctuary with me. Come to the Squat and Gobble Lodge, Road 156, Lickstrap, Louisiana."*

"I had some strange talks with this man. He is a survivalist and believes the government in fact, all governments are out to take control of everyone," Violet said.

"Sounds a little like us," I said.

"He is one of the men who claimed to have been rescued by Curtis."

"Curtis, otherwise believed to be Dranco. This could be our break. If Dranco escaped from Opus 8, it would make sense he would contact one of the last men to have seen him, someone he felt he could trust," Zandra said.

"Plus, this lodge is close, just outside the quarantined boundaries on open water, according to my GPS," Violet added.

"Violet, you and Ed head out to the Squat and Gobble Grill and Lodge. Richard and I will join you later. It will take a day to drive there. On the way, Violet, you can fill Ed in about Curtis and Crazy Willie. Richard and I should arrive shortly after you guys do," Zandra said.

The next day, we left for Louisiana our destination: the Squat and Gobble, and Crazy Willie's cabin. The cabin was located on the edge of Gauthier's Bayou. Violet and I drove for a few hours before she started to explain our connection to Crazy Willie.

"I searched online and heard about a couple of local legends. One stood out: Crazy Willie. Crazy Willie sent you the letter. Once that letter was received, he knew we would be on our way. That was our agreement. He is very secretive. He'll be there, along with his grandmother. They own the grill and lodge together. He was the last known person to have had contact with Curtis," she said.

"Have you met in person?" I asked.

"No, everything was done online or briefly on the phone." "What did you tell him?"

"That we are doing research for a book on paranormal events and the ghost story about Curtis. I'm your assistant." Violet smiled, then continued. "There is a folktale about a man named Curtis. No last name. According to the story, he grew up in the inner swamps with his parents and grandparents. Curtis would come into town every so often to get basic supplies and then just disappear back into the swamps. The townspeople knew Curtis well. He was never considered a threat to anyone. After some time, the town began to grow. There was talk of turning the swamplands into federal lands. It would help the economy of the town tremendously. The mayor had the sheriff and his posse of twenty men take boats out to Curtis's shack. They were to peacefully remove him from his homestead in order for the deal to go through with the federal government."

49

"It must have been tragic for Curtis," I said.

"Actually, he was the only survivor, according to the folktales," she said.

"What happened?"

"Curtis took a stand and refused to leave. There was a scuffle, shots were fired, and by the next morning, Curtis was the only one left alive."

"How many were killed?" I asked.

"Twenty-one men in total, including the sheriff. They never found any bodies. Curtis was ninety-three years old when that happened. That was over eighty years ago. Word has it that he's been spotted numerous times by local hunters. Crazy Willie says he knows where Curtis's shack is located. He says Curtis helped him find his way out about a year ago," she said.

"Curtis must be a ghost, or he is almost 170 years old," I said. "Or he is a reptilian shape-shifter by the name of Dranco,"

Violet added.

We pulled into the Squat and Gobble. Some of the colorful locals were hanging outside the place. I noticed one of the bigger guys mutter something.

"So you're a Yankee, Ed?" Violet asked, smiling.

"Leftover animosity from our Civil War. You know, the North against the South."

Just then, one of the other men spoke up. "It's closed." I looked over at him. He looked as dumb as he was big.

"Are you stupid, boy, or just looking for trouble?" he asked. "Neither, gentlemen. We are looking for Crazy Willie." Violet

stepped out of the car, her long hair gently blowing in the slight breeze. She looked and walked like a model. She had these rednecks in the palm of her hand.

She looked at the biggest one and smiled. "You haven't seen him, have you? You look like someone a girl could trust," she said and smiled at the men as she talked.

It was fun to watch. They were about to settle some old Civil War grudges just a few seconds ago, and now they were all drooling over Violet.

"Depends. You aren't cops, are ya?" the large redneck asked.

The front door opened up, and a short pear-shaped gray-haired woman came out. She had a bright yellow apron that had the words "You heard me right. Shut up and eat your grits."

"You boys, get. You're scaring away my only customers. Come on in, you two. I got plenty of sweet tea, beer, and some of Crazy Willie's Bayou Moonshine. By the way, I'm Miss Linda, Willie's grandma," she said.

"I'm Violet Conway, and this is Ed Pinley," Violet said.

"Oh, I knows all about you two. Crazy Willie's been talking about this book you all are writing," Miss Linda said.

"That's right," I started to say as we followed her into the diner. We were the only ones in there. She reached under the counter and came up with a dusty bottle and a sawed-off shotgun. I looked at Violet in disbelief.

"Don't bother yourself none with this here gun. It's just habit, I guess. I never drink Crazy Willie's Moonshine unless I got Maybell with me," Miss Linda said. She patted her gunstock affectionately. She reached under the bar, got three small canning jars, and filled them up halfway. "To Crazy Willie and that damn swamp thing or monster or whatever it is!" she toasted.

Violet picked up her glass and joined in with Miss Linda, slamming the whole thing down in one motion.

"Damn, she was thirsty. Listen, sweetheart, you help yourself to as much as you want." Miss Linda pushed the bottle over toward Violet, looked at me, and winked. "You'll both need a room for the night. Crazy Willie won't be back till morning." She got up and headed for the kitchen doors.

Violet reached over, picked up my glass, and slammed it. "Whoopee, that is good moonshine, Miss Linda!" she said.

"We got plenty where that came from, little lady. I got catfish on the grill, coming right up," Miss Linda replied as she walked through the kitchen doors.

"I know you don't drink, so I helped you out," Violet said. "Thanks. I didn't want to offend her," I said. To my disbelief, Violet picked the bottle up and poured two more glasses.

"Miss Linda is sweet. I like her and Crazy Willie's Moonshine," she said.

She downed my glass and set it in front of me. Miss Linda came out with heaping plates of Southern hospitality. She placed them in front of us.

"I see you like your moonshine too, young man. You both take it easy now. That stuff sneaks up on ya. Now you'll each need a room for the night, am I right?"

"Yes, ma'am," I said.

"Good, 'cause I don't see no ring. You aren't married, so I fixed Ed a room upstairs. It's comfortable, plenty of breeze. Honey, I got your room ready as well."

A few minutes later, Miss Linda appeared at our table with good news. "After you all finish your catfish, I got a surprise for ya. You two just wait. I got dessert. Miss Linda's tuna fish lime Jell-O bars coming right up, just the way Crazy Willie likes 'em," she said. She then strolled back into her kitchen to retrieve the dessert.

I looked at Violet. She had finished her third glass of moonshine and was reaching for the fourth.

"Dang, this is good, Eddie." Violet was smiling as she slammed the rest down in one gulp. She was developing a Southern drawl with each glass. She was obviously getting hammered. Then I noticed that her skin color was changing; she was becoming darker in tone.

"Violet, are you all right?" I asked.

She was smiling, and then she turned. She turned into Violet, her real shape-shifter self. She had grayish skin, with multiple colors flaring out around her ears and forehead. Her body shape was very much that of a human but much larger. Her eyes were larger and a bit wider apart. They were beautiful large eyes. Then she blinked.

"Violet, are you all right?" I asked again. "Why, Eddie?"

"You seem to be shape-shifting. Miss Linda is going to be right out," I said.

"Oh no. Sorry, Eddie. I'll try to keep it under control."

I watched as Violet shifted back to her human form. Just then, Miss Linda came through the kitchen's swinging doors.

"Here you two go." Miss Linda placed two plates of tuna fish lime Jell-O bars in front of us, along with two bowls of boiled peanuts. "This here is Crazy Willie's favorite dessert. He's my grandson. Hell, me and Crazy Willie started this here boarding house/restaurant twenty years ago. I keep to this place, and Willie, he's an outfitter, takes people fishing for money. I can't believe people are so dumb they pay Crazy Willie to take them fishing. But they do!" she said.

Violet laughed. I looked at her. She was changing colors again. Miss Linda didn't notice as she made her way back into her kitchen. The kitchen's swinging doors were getting a workout.

"Violet."

"Yes, Eddie."

"You are turning again." "Oops, sorry. I slipped."

Violet gained her human color back as Miss Linda came out with a cigar box. She opened it and held it out to me. "Care for a cigar, Mr. Pinley?"

"Oh yes, I'd love one too, Miss Linda," Violet said.

Miss Linda was smiling at Violet. "You got spunk, girl. Heck, I'll join you all," she said.

We had finished off the dessert and were enjoying our cigars on the front porch. The night breeze was warm, and the sky was bright with stars.

"You know about what happened a few years back?" Miss Linda looked at us and began her story. "My grandson, Crazy Willie, and twelve or so men went after that swamp monster. It almost cost all of them their lives. They were gone almost five days. We all gave up on them, when the dumb sons of guns showed up one morning. Everyone made it back in one piece, but they didn't say a lot. Something happened out there. Willie will tell ya when he gets back. None of those guys have come around here looking for Willie since that happened. You going to put Willie's story in your book?" she asked.

"Maybe. We are writing a book about ghost stories. This story about Curtis fits right in. Willie sent Ed a letter," Violet replied.

"I know. I mailed it for him. He's been kind of strange lately. Not that anyone else would notice, but I do. He's going through his meat pretty fast, more than one man's rations. And he's gone away a lot," Miss Linda added.

"You say he'll be back tomorrow?" Violet asked.

"Yes, dear. Now you all relax here by the fire. I'll be right back." Miss Linda left the room.

"Wonder how Crazy Willie earned his name?" I asked.

"I asked Willie that the last time we talked. He just laughed," Violet said.

"Miss Linda seems concerned. She says he's eating a lot of meat, or someone is," I said.

"And he's gone a lot."

Miss Linda entered the room with an armful of fresh towels. "Now you two must be exhausted. Here, honey, I'll show you to your room. Ed, your room is upstairs, right around the corner, first door on the right." She handed me my towel set.

"Now, honey, you better get some shut eye. Willie will be here early." Miss Linda and Violet walked off.

I was left alone with lots of questions. One of the questions that rattled around my brain was, why do they call him Crazy Willie? I tossed and turned all night, finally falling asleep at 3:30 a.m.

The next morning, I woke up to someone singing very badly. I listened carefully to hear the words; I was barely able to recognize the melody. The man kept singing.

"What do you get when you fall in love? Herpes, scabies, and gonorrhea. A wet handshake, and then it's 'I'll see ya.' I'll never fall in love again. I'll never fall in love again," the man sang.

It was that big ending that finally got Miss Linda's attention. "Willie, those aren't the words to that song. You sing it right, or I'll"

"You'll do what, Miss Linda? You said you liked my voice," Crazy Willie said.

"I like your voice just fine, Willie. All I'm asking is you learn the right words," she said.

Miss Linda went back into the lodge. I watched as the man she called Willie walked into the walk-in deep freezer. Soon he came out with several packages of meat. He also held a package that looked like it came from a pharmacy. The man then walked into the lodge.

I decided to join them after I had a nice long cold shower. I was sweating buckets already; it was going to be hot. Violet sat at the table, talking with the man I saw outside. It was Willie.

"Good morning, Ed. This is Willie," Violet said as she and Willie stood up.

"Good morning. It's nice to put a face to the voice, Mr. Pinley," Willie said.

"Call me Ed."

"I'm Willie Gauthier. The books and the pamphlets you sent me paid off."

"How so, Willie?"

"Well, this guy I'm helping out recognized you, Miss Violet. I had a pamphlet with me about your ghost investigations," Willie said.

"Who is he, Willie?" Violet asked.

"He's the man they say is a ghost. They call him Curtis. I assure you, he ain't no ghost. He eats like he's starving. He saved my life. I figured I owed him one, so I gave him refuge and told him that I would bring Miss Violet to him," Willie said.

"Wait a minute, Willie. I need to go as well," I said.

"You'll be close by. I'm sure he will want to meet you as well. It turns out Miss Violet and Curtis go way back."

"It's true, Willie. I may know him, but I won't know until I see him. I'm a doctor as well, Willie. What is in the pharmacy bag?" Violet asked.

"Penicillin and some other things. He got himself injured pretty badly."

"How bad?"

"Some deep cuts. Should have got stitches, but he refused. He can't see a doctor, and he is running from the law. I think he's running from

56

them." He pointed to the sky as two black helicopters flew overhead. "We can go see him after the skies calm down."

Willie shook my hand and excused himself. He and Miss Linda went into the kitchen.

"Does Dranco know your human form, Violet?" I asked.

"Yes. As a government worker, I had to reveal my shape-shifting abilities. Dranco personally looked through a series of holograms of deceased humans. He picked out my human shape, and I had to replicate that human shape. Ever since then, I've used this human form," Violet said.

"Well, let's have a drink with Willie and see what we can learn," I said.

"You don't drink," Violet said.

"I know, but, girl, you can. Besides, Willie is sweet on ya." "Oh please, Ed."

I grabbed her hand, and we entered the lodge. "Willie, can we buy you a drink?" I asked.

"Sure. You got time for a little history lesson?" Willie asked. "Sure, we always have time for history stories."

"More than stories, Ed. What I'm going to tell you really happened to us. We saw it all happen right in front of us. Our hunting party reached Brite's Point. From there, we paddled our way into the swamp. The way seemed clear. I had gone hunting back there years ago. We were armed to the teeth and gunning for that monster gator. We were into the second day when we were first made aware of the monster's presence. During the night, that gator came onshore and destroyed our boats and most of our gear and provisions. It ripped the boats in half, leaving just splinters floating on top of the water," Willie said.

"Did you see the gator?" I asked.

"No. None of us did. If we had seen it, we would have killed it. We were hunting for it, but really, it was hunting us. The guys with me were shaken up. We all were. Fact was, we were deep in the swamp, surrounded by water, with no boat to get out. We decided to walk as far as we could, staying out of the water as much as possible. We were lost for days. I couldn't figure it out. We must have been going in circles.

"The whole time, I could feel that thing looking at us, following us, but still staying hidden. Then it appeared, its head just barely above the waterline. Mike and another guy were in the water, trying to cross over to another island, when the gator started to swim toward them. We all thought they were dead meat," Willie said.

"What happened?" I asked.

"Nothing. That really bothered us. We realized it was tracking us, hunting us, waiting for its chance to get all of us at once. It was like it was playing with us, almost like a cat does with its catch just before killing it.

"It was dusk when we noticed the activity. There were gators all around, more than normal. We could hear them swishing their tails. Seemed like there were twenty-five or more just offshore. They surfaced, allowing us to see them. Then an old man appeared.

"He paddled up to us and stayed just offshore. From his boat, he commanded the gators to swim toward us. The gators slowly started to arrive onshore and circled us, just ten feet away. Then he commanded them to stand down, and they did. The gators watched us while the man spoke. He told us that he had two boats for us and that he would guide us out safely."

"He didn't ask for anything?" Violet asked.

"No. In fact, he said that if we stayed away and left him alone, that would be pay enough. That was last year, just before hurricane season. Last week, that same man showed up at my base camp. He was hurt. I managed to dress his wound and stop the bleeding. Now he needs your help, Miss Violet. He said you could get him out of here safely, to his own kind. I know what he is. I've heard the stories of the skin-walker. Hell, I seen it myself," Willie said.

"We can help. Let's go," Violet said.

We all climbed into Miss Linda's SUV and proceeded to drive to Willie's base camp. Violet was on her phone while we drove. It was a forty-minute drive on rock and sand along the bayou shoreline. We reached the base camp; it was very rustic. There was an old vintage RV Winnebago camper hidden under a camouflage tarp.

"Ed, go on inside and wait. We will be back soon. There is cold iced tea, maybe some beer inside, and it's air-conditioned," Crazy Willie said. I was good with cold iced tea and air-conditioning. I waited inside and watched through the small window as Willie and Violet walked off into the brush.

It had been at least thirty minutes when Violet came to the camper door. "Zandra and Richard will be here anytime now. It appears that it is Dranco. We need to get him to our base," she said.

"How is he?"

"Cut up pretty bad. He got caught in their nets. He cut himself out just before they raised the nets. He left them that decoy with a bomb in it. There's more. He is now in his reptilian form and must remain that way to heal."

"How are we going to transport him? He must be huge," I said. "Zandra and Richard have taken care of that problem," Violet replied.

Just then, I heard the air brakes of a large tractor trailer parking outside. I walked to the window and saw two men walking toward the RV. Violet opened the door.

"Is this Crazy Willie's Outfitters?" one of the men asked.

"Sure is." Willie walked up to the RV. "I'm Willie. This here is Miss Conway and Mr. Pinley."

"We are here to transport your giant alligator, sir."

I looked at the tractor trailer outside. Written on it in bold letters was "Uncle Lope's Cajun Carnival Featuring: The World's Largest Living Alligator."

"Willie and I will get the alligator ready," Violet said.

"We have some equipment in the rig. I'll get it ready." The shorter one of the two limped off to get his gear.

"What happened to him?" I asked the other man. "He got bit in the leg last week," the man said.

"Your job must be dangerous. What was it, a snake or something?" I asked.

"Naw, his girlfriend's poodle doesn't like him. The little bastard bites him every time he comes over."

The short guy drove a small tractor-type vehicle, carrying a large tank. The tractor maneuvered down the trail slowly for a few hundred feet until they reached the spot Willie was standing at.

Willie had the two men walk back to the tractor trailer. He explained that it would be safer for them to keep some distance between them and the giant alligator, in case it broke loose. He told them that last year, the damn thing got three of his men before they could sedate it. They hurried off toward the tractor trailer.

I watched as the water started to bubble, then I saw a large reptilian creature emerge from the murky water. The reptilian they called Dranco limped as he approached the container, and then he entered it. I barely caught a glimpse of the huge creature. The two men cautiously returned and loaded the container into the covered trailer. Willie brought a water hose over and connected it to the trailer input. Richard and Zandra walked over to us.

"Miss Linda called. Said some government vehicles are in the area. They rolled by the Squat and Gobble about two minutes ago. They are on the way," Zandra said.

"How much time do we have?" Violet asked. "Ten minutes maybe."

"Okay. Ed and I will follow the truck out. You guys ready?" Violet asked.

Richard and the two men disconnected the water hose and climbed up into their truck. They slowly exited onto the dirt road. Zandra, Violet, and I drove a few miles, then the tractor trailer turned onto another unmarked road. We followed the narrow road until the semi stopped. We were out of sight of the main road. We turned everything off and stood silently, listening as four black SUVs flew by.

"I hope Willie knows what to say," I said.

"He does. We briefed him, and he's capable of pulling it off. He'll show them where he saw the creature dive into the water. We left plenty of footprints and evidence around. The government divers will discover the underwater cavern where Dranco has been recovering from his wounds," Zandra said.

"What about Willie? They might figure out he helped us," Violet said.

"Richard took care of that. While we were getting the rig ready, he made a call to the local sheriff. He impersonated Willie and told the sheriff he thought he saw something outside his hunting shack. He thought it was that alligator man everyone's been seeing," she said. "Well, it took the sheriff a while to decide to call the Feds. He thought Willie was messing with him. That gave us enough time to get out."

After a while, she said, "Looks clear. Let's head out. I bet they will be quite busy for some time."

We all got back into our vehicles and proceeded toward the state highway and then west. Zandra and Richard rode with the two men. They headed south for the coast with the semitruck. Violet and I headed northwest to our home.

On the way, we talked about everything under the sun. We planned out the new book dealing with the real threat of reptilian creatures from other dimensions, the secret world government cover-ups, and native ghost stories from around the world.

We had found Dranco. It had been important to the team to bring him in, and we did it. As we got closer to our apartment, Violet became quiet.

"Is everything all right? You seem sad," I said.

"I'm a little sad, Ed. I will miss working with you," she said. "What do you mean?" I asked.

"I'm being called back."

"Then you won't be my assistant any longer?"

"I've made arrangements, and I have your new assistant in place already. Everything will go on as it always has," she said.

"What do I do? How do I get a hold of anyone?"

"If you are needed, we will contact you. Your assistant is one of our best," she added.

"When do you leave, Violet?"

"I've already left, Ed. Goodbye, my friend."

I looked over, and I could see that Violet was a hologram. She indeed had already left. The last bit of her light essence vanished before my eyes.

I wondered how long she had been gone and replaced by her hologram. We had been talking for quite some time, and I couldn't tell it was her hologram. I wondered if her hologram had been there when we all split up. Zandra, Richard, and Violet had gone south with Dranco. Violet's hologram and I had gone north. I kind of felt like the redheaded stepchild for a little while. Then I started thinking about my conversation with Violet the night before.

She was right; we had accomplished a lot. We did it without casualties. Dranco was now safe, and the nuclear threat from the

Rufilian was over. Opus 8—well, there may be some sour feelings among some of their rank and file.

As I drove, I wondered what Violet's replacement would be like. She had mentioned that she already had my assistant in place and that everything had already been taken care of. I smiled as I thought of this last adventure with Zandra and the team—especially Violet. I already missed her.

Chapter 7

The Assistant

I was looking forward to meeting my new assistant. Violet had assured me I would be pleased with the new candidate. I wondered what the new assistant would look like. Maybe the candidate would turn out to be a tall blond or a redhead. I was hoping for someone like Violet—kind, fun, and very organized. With her, I never had to deal with any business issues. Needless to say, I was excited to meet the new assistant.

I dropped off the rental SUV and caught the bus to my apartment. From the bus stop two blocks away, I approached my building. I walked up the stone steps to my door. I put the key in the lock and turned it. I was immediately surprised to see my apartment filled with cigarette smoke. I looked around and saw half of the local homeless population sitting around my apartment, drinking what was apparently the last of my homemade root beer. There were empty bags of potato chips and Cheetos mixed in with cigarette butts all over my wood floor.

"I'm Chester Mosley, your new assistant. Mr. Pinley, we don't have a lot of time. Agents Frost and Henderson will be here soon. They intend to arrest you. Now if you follow me, I'll show you to your safe room." Standing in front of me was a short, slightly overweight balding man with bright-green eyes and a crooked smile. My new assistant!

"Chester, why are these people here?"

"Distractions, sir. Zandra said that their presence here would confuse the authorities," Chester replied.

"Chester, they are swigging down the last of my homemade root beer."

"Yes, sir. They overwhelmed the refrigerator and had their way with everything in there before I could stop them," he said.

"Distractions. Chester, really, I don't think I should run from the law," I said.

Before my eyes, Chester became me. He certainly was a shapeshifter. "Now, sir, I'll show you to your room."

I followed him to a small closet. "Chester, you do realize this is a small closet. I hardly use it."

"Yes, sir."

He waved his hand. A shimmering blue light appeared, and the wall opened up. We walked into a large room. It was completely furnished.

"You can wait here, sir. Zandra and Richard will arrive soon." "Chester, what's with all the commotion?"

"Your book, sir. Apparently, you wrote about some things that were previously top secret and unknown. So they have a lot of questions to ask you."

"How do you know they're coming to arrest us? I mean you. Or me. Whatever."

"Richard caught wind of this through screening communications between Opus 8 and some high-ranking members of the US government. I'll be you, and while they are busy interrogating me posing as you, Ed Pinley, you and the team can safely wait this out. Now we don't have a lot of time, sir. Do be careful."

"Where are you going, Chester?"

"Agents Henderson and Frost are coming here to arrest you. I must be available for them as you." Chester smiled and closed the door, and the wall closed behind him, leaving me alone.

I looked around the room. It was exactly like my apartment. The only difference was, there were no working doorknobs. There was no way out. I walked over to the window to look out. It was fake as well; I was in a doorless, windowless room.

Chester had said that Zandra and Richard would be arriving soon, so I decided to chill. He had also said something about my new book. I looked around and found a copy of the most recently published book, The Secret World Government and the Elimination of the Reptilian Threat.

As soon as I read the title, I remembered everything in that book as if I had actually written it. Violet was the gifted writer; I had just thrown out ideas. Now I understood why Frost and Henderson were here to question me.

I sat back on the couch and began to think about Violet. I already missed her.

I must have fallen asleep, and I began to dream. It seemed so real. I was dreaming that Violet and I were having dinner at the Squat and Gobble. Violet took my hand, looked at me, and began to kiss me passionately.

"Ed, Ed, are you all right?" Zandra asked.

"Zandra, his face is twitching or something. Ed, wake up," Richard said.

I opened my eyes. My beautiful dream dwindled away as I realized I was being observed by Zandra and Richard.

"So here we are. It seems like it was just yesterday. I didn't know I had this room. I didn't know it was even here," I said.

"This room does not exist in our dimension. This room exists in a dimension that is in coexistence with our dimension. The difference between dimensions is our development in culture, science, medicine, or social condition. This dimension or any other dimension we may visit will differ drastically from one another," Zandra said.

"We created a distraction with your book release. So while you're being investigated by Washington, we plan to take the world's most dangerous man out," Richard said.

"What do you mean by 'out'?" I asked.

"This mission will be unlike any other, Ed. We have been ordered to use any force necessary to stop this threat. We have three days to find and eliminate Himmler Furling. He is a World Science Foundation member in charge of the international research center in Moscow," Zandra said.

"That sounds harmless enough," I said.

"Yes, except he is close to discovering the portal equation. If he does, he will do what the Rufilian tried to do use it as a weapon to conquer earth and then other dimensions. We need to find Himmler Furling and take him out of the equation. We have been authorized to use lethal means if necessary. We have not killed anyone since we arrived here over four hundred years ago," Richard said.

"We devised a plan to capture Himmler Furling and transfer him to another dimension. There he will be harmless, unable to recreate his concept in that world. He will sound like a madman who's out of his mind. It's a prison like no other. He will be held back by the reality of things in that dimension. He will be in a prison with no walls and no escape. We won't have to kill him," Zandra said, smiling.

"So some dimensions are more advanced than others. Are we time-traveling?" I asked.

"Time remains the same in each dimension. You cannot time travel. That is physically impossible. But you can enter other dimensions. All dimensions are on the same time wave. It is like showing ten movies at the same time on a giant screen each movie is different in every way from the other movies, but all the movies are playing at the same time. Everyone interacting in their movie, their reality is happening in real time for them at the same time as all the other movies are playing, with each group of actors following their script or plot. If you were to leave your movie and enter another movie, you would not be time-traveling into that movie. You would be entering the movie at the moment you entered. Time-traveling has nothing to do with it. You enter it at the time you do. So each dimension is different not because of time but because of the human condition in each dimension and the natural conditions that prevail."

"So what happens now?"

"Violet is in Moscow now and has our target under surveillance. She has recorded every movement Himmler Furling has made in the last few days. We will create a plan to snatch Himmler and transfer him back here," Zandra said.

"You're going to bring Himmler back to this safe room?"

"This room is not what it seems to be, Ed. We are in a dimension that is far behind our world, as far as the human condition or natural conditions go. Outside of this structure is a very different world from ours. It is a wasteland inhabited by what appear to be wandering tribes. We are hidden from any observers by what appears to them to be rocky cliffs. We have the comfort of this apartment inside the rocky cliffs, but outside, the inhabitants of this world have a very different existence from ours in this room. It will be out there that we will place Mr. Himmler," Richard said.

"When do we meet up with Violet?" I asked.

"We will meet up with Violet and kidnap Himmler Furling before the genius achieves his goal. Once he is transported back here, we will release him like a wild animal into his new environment just outside this apartment. Case closed. Ed, you'll meet up with Violet and help capture Himmler Furling. In two hours, you'll fly to Moscow. Stay put at the airport until Violet contacts you. From there, you and Violet will orchestrate the kidnapping of a very famous scientist. Are you ready for this?" Zandra asked.

"As ready as ever. What does this guy look like?" I asked. "Here are the most recent pictures of Himmler Furling. He does the same thing every day. At 5:30 a.m., he goes to the office and doesn't stop anywhere for food or coffee. At 11:00 a.m., his car arrives, and he is driven to a private bathhouse. He is not sighted leaving the bathhouse, but every morning, he is sighted leaving for work at 5:30 a.m. from his home," Richard said.

"So somehow he is able to travel unobserved from the bathhouse to his home," I said.

"Yes, that's right. You and Violet need to grab him during that time. You have two minutes to transport Himmler Furling before they know he is gone," Zandra said.

"Is there security or anything we need to know about?"

"We know the bathhouse is private, members only. Security is tight. Drugs and girls anything you want can be purchased, no questions asked," Richard said.

"How do we get in?" I asked.

"No problem. Violet just got hired today. She will be Himmler's plaything for Thursday night. They will send a car to pick her up and take her to the bathhouse once he requests her presence. Once there, she will be escorted into Himmler Furling's room. You will be in an ambulance parked one block away. Wait for Violet's 911 call for medical assistance. She will say that Himmler Furling is having a heart attack. You will arrive with the ambulance and transport Himmler Furling and Violet. Just around the first corner is a private gated parking garage. The gate will be up. You drive into the parking garage, and Zandra and I will be waiting," Richard said.

"What's our exit plan?"

"Working on that. It's complicated. But while the police and the real ambulance are going to the bathhouse, we will transport Furling out of the bathhouse into the parking garage. From there, we meet up with a helicopter and return to the States with Himmler Furling," Zandra said.

I got ready for my flight to Moscow to meet up with Violet. I hoped this really was Violet and not her hologram. Although I must say, I really could not tell the difference between her and her hologram while riding in the truck or during the rescue of Dranco. I boarded my flight and took a catnap on the way.

We landed and started to deplane. Outside, I could see a few people standing on the sideway. Violet was nowhere to be seen. I walked down the stairs and was abruptly greeted by two men dressed in black two-piece suits. They each grabbed an arm, and we gingerly made our way to an open door leading down a set of steel spiral steps. At the bottom of the stairs, there was a dimly lit room.

"Sit down," one of the men said. I looked over to where the voice had come from, only to be greeted by a four-finger knuckle sandwich. I saw stars like I had never seen before. They danced all around, up and down, and they were the brightest stars I had ever seen.

The stars started swirling around in symmetrical patterns, becoming brighter and brighter. Then I just sat there, holding my precious teddy bear.

"Ed, Ed, wake up," Violet said.

I thought I heard something, but I was busy trying to stuff white cotton balls back into my teddy bear's forehead, which had split open.

"Ed, come on. We need to go." Somehow I heard a voice drawing me back; it was Violet's voice.

"What? Oh, my head," I moaned. "Ed, we need to go now."

I looked up out of one eye and saw Violet standing over me with an extended arm. I reached up and grabbed it. She pulled me to my feet.

"When did you get here?" I asked.

"I've been here a while. I was one of the two men who intercepted you. Sorry about the punch in the face, but I didn't know how else to disable the other guy with me. Once you hit the ground, he bent over to check you, and I gave him a little shot. He's sleeping it off now," Violet said with a smile.

We made our way through what seemed to be the maintenance tunnel until we reached a large metal door. Violet slowly opened it up, revealing the alley behind a large stone building. I could hear the planes taxiing not far from us. We walked for a few blocks. There was a Volkswagen parked, with its motor running.

"Get in, Ed."

Violet got behind the wheel. We pulled away and headed toward the older, poorer side of town. We parked on a side street and got out. We made our way along a garbage-littered path leading to a small cottage. Violet knocked on the door, and it slowly opened. She walked in. I followed.

Once inside, she turned toward me and smiled. "It's good to see you again, Ed, even if it hasn't been that long."

"I agree, Violet. You are the real Violet, right?" I asked.

"Yes, I'm real." She leaned over and kissed my cheek. "Now let's get ready. Here is your EMT uniform. The ambulance will be parked one block west. Get in and wait for my call. Right now, I'm waiting for my car to arrive to pick up my hologram at Maxwell's. When the car arrives, I'll be there."

"What is Maxwell's?"

"A gentlemen's club. My hologram is dancing for them as we speak. After the private dance session, I'm supposed to be picked up at eleven

71

thirty. My hologram will be dancing. When she is done dancing, I, the real Violet, will take over." She smiled as she took my hand and led me to the door. "Show starts in one hour. That will give you plenty of time to reach the parked ambulance. Meanwhile, I need to get ready. Here's the address and map to where the ambulance is parked. Also, your EMT uniform is in this bag."

"Violet, be careful." I felt uneasy about this. She winked at me and closed the door.

I made my way through the back streets, keeping an eye out for anything unusual. The night air smelled good. I could hear groups of people laughing. I stopped at a street crossing and charted my route. I needed to cross this street and head five blocks east.

I crossed over. Just as I stepped off the curb, a car descended on me. I jumped out of the way just in time. I looked back, and two men got out of the car, their guns drawn. I looked up and saw there was a balcony, so I climbed onto it. Then I jumped and landed on the porch next door. I jumped again, this time to an adjacent rooftop, and I was gone. I was surprised by my agility and ability to jump that high.

I made my way along the rooftops until I found a good area to wait it out for a spell. I listened for police activity. There was no activity; my attackers were not police. I recharted my route. I was now pushing it for time. I needed to get a move on. I could run fast, but I had to be careful on these back streets. I started running at a brisk pace. The streets were dark; I didn't see them hiding by the side of the road.

"Stop, or we will kill you."

I looked over and saw three men holding bats. They were locals, and they looked hungry. I stopped. "I'm in a hurry, gentlemen," I said. bag."

"Shut up and hand over your wallet and whatever is in that They approached, lifting their bats up above their heads. That was their first and final mistake.

A few seconds later, I was on my way. I really don't know what occurred, but I was beginning to like these implants. I rounded the corner. The ambulance was parked right where it was supposed to be. I waited and watched. I still had three minutes before I had to be inside the ambulance. I found some trees and changed into my EMT uniform behind them. I walked over and got into the ambulance and waited for Violet's call.

The call came, and I made my way to the entrance. The guard was waiting for me; they had Himmler Furling on a gurney. Violet was standing next to him. I wheeled the gurney over to the ambulance, and we loaded Himmler Furling in. Violet got in as well. I pulled away and headed toward the private parking lot. We could hear the ambulance and three Russian police cars coming our way. We turned into our private parking lot. A few minutes later, the ambulance and police rushed by.

"Good job, Ed. Let's get Himmler Furling out of here," Violet said.

We rolled Himmler Furling out of the ambulance. He looked like he was out cold.

"He is alive, right?" I asked.

"Oh yes, very alive. When he wakes, I'm sure he won't be as frisky as he was. I may have broken a couple ribs defending myself," she said.

"You okay?" I asked.

"Oh, yes. I hate to say it, but I enjoyed putting him in his place. I'm also looking forward to putting him in his place again. Zandra said to abandon the ambulance. There is a Suburban waiting over here."

We carried Himmler Furling over and dumped him in the back. I started to get in, but Violet stopped me. "We get into this one next to it," she said.

We got in, and she started the car. A few seconds later, two people I had never seen before got in the Suburban and drove off. We followed, making our way toward the outskirts of Moscow.

Two hours later, we stopped along the highway. Off in the distance I could hear a helicopter coming our way. One of the two men who drove the Suburban approached us. As he came closer, I could see that it was Richard, and Zandra was close by.

"Violet will take you to the airport, Ed. We will all meet up at your apartment in a few days. Be careful, Ed. It's not quite over yet," Zandra said.

She and Richard loaded Himmler Furling into the landed helicopter. They both boarded it, and it slowly lifted up off the ground and disappeared into the night sky.

"We better get going. Your plane leaves soon," Violet said. "Are you Violet or her hologram?"

She let out a soft laugh. "I'm her, the real Violet." She leaned over and kissed me softly on the cheek and then on the lips. "Shall we go, Ed?"

I was in shock. I had been waiting for this moment for quite some time, and it all happened so fast that I missed it.

"Ed, you okay?" Violet asked.

"Yes, yes, I'm fine. Couldn't be finer," I said.

She laughed and started to drive toward the airport.

I thought about what just went down. It seemed too easy. We had just kidnapped the world's smartest man because he was the world's most dangerous man. I wondered if the authorities had any idea what happened to Himmler Furling. I turned on the radio; of course, it was in Russian.

"Violet, do you understand Russian?" I asked.

"Yes." She reached over and turned the dial and listened. "It's the news. Nothing so far."

I could hear Zandra's voice in the back of my head. *"Be careful, Ed. It's not quite over yet."*

Ahead of us was the road check we had gone through earlier. We were waved over, and a guard approached us. Violet spoke to him in fluent Russian. They laughed, and he pointed to a parking spot. She walked back.

"Are we being detained?" I asked.

"No, they just have to verify my papers. He called his captain," she said.

"This is probably bad, right?" I asked.

The guard approached us, smiling. He and Violet talked for a few minutes, then he handed her a card key pass. She got in and started the car, and we drove off, silent for a few miles.

When she finally spoke, she said, "The guard said our flights are canceled until further notice. Also, there is a manhunt for Himmler Furling and his kidnappers. We've been directed to go to Customs at the airport. There will be soldiers waiting for us."

We arrived to a group of well-armed soldiers. They opened our doors, and we were escorted into a black Suburban. We drove and then parked in front of a nineteenth-century mansion. Once we were inside, the soldiers departed. Two men dressed in three-piece suits approached us.

"Ed Pinley and Violet Conway, it's a pleasure to meet you both.

Will you both please come this way?"

The taller man led the way. We entered the elevator and traveled to the top floor. The elevator doors opened. In front of us was a beautiful water fountain with multiple waterfalls. There were pools with koi fish, statues, and sculptures; there was visual art everywhere.

"Come this way."

We followed the tall man through a large door. He spoke into a box, and the second door swung open. We walked inside. It was dark. In front of us was a large table.

Someone sat at the head of the table. There were lights at his back, shining outward and making it impossible to see his face.

"Mr. Pinley, Miss Conway, make yourselves comfortable. Please be seated," the tall man said.

We sat, keeping our eyes on the man we could not see clearly because of the lights. All around us, the lights slowly became brighter, highlighting the man in front of us.

Before us sat Himmler Furling, who was grinning from ear to ear. He stood up.

"I kept you both alive so that I could show you the future you and all your friends are trying to stop. You and your pathetic group of misfits have no chance. You can't stop me now. Look how easy it was to fool all of you. You thought you had Himmler Furling. Instead, you got my double. By now, your people know that they don't have Himmler Furling. Also, they know we have you two. They probably think that I will react like the animals they are and kill you both. They are wrong. I'm a peaceful man. I only want to make money. I want to be a pioneer."

He got up and walked around his large table. He peered at Violet, his eyes large and blazing. "Violet, you fear us using the portal to invade other dimensions, perhaps places where us humans have an advantage. You should be afraid, very afraid. I have plans for hunting expeditions. I just have to find the right dimensions. We plan to turn every place we can into a settlement and begin trading. The advantage will be unlimited. Look at the money and power we will have by cornering the market early."

"I'd say it's early, Furling. All you have is a dream. You don't have the device needed to activate the energy field. You might have the formula to create the energy field, but without the device, you're stuck," Violet said. There seemed to be a change in her temperament. I could tell she did not like what Furling was up to.

"You're right, Violet, we don't quite have the device. We are close, so close. We can now experiment with our prototype. My scientist says they may be ready to test the device tomorrow morning. You both should get some rest. Morning comes early," Himmler said. Two soldiers accompanied us to our rooms. They locked the doors and stood guard outside. I looked at the windows; they had bars. There was a searchlight that swept the area along our wall every few seconds. I looked around the room and spotted two cameras. I was sure there were listening devices as well. Going to sleep would be hard, but I was going to try.

Morning did come early. The knocks on my door interrupted my dream. I was swimming with Violet. We were swimming in crystal-blue water; it was warm and refreshing. She turned toward me when the knocks on my door interrupted my dream.

"Yes," I answered.

"Mr. Furling requests your presence for breakfast. You have thirty minutes to get ready," the voice said.

"Thank you," I said.

I got up and found the shower. It was completely stocked with everything I needed. When I finished showering, there were clothes laid out for me on my bed. I dressed in the furnished clothes.

"Mr. Pinley," the voice said. "Yes, I'm ready."

"Good, sir. Mr. Furling is excited. He's been looking forward to this for weeks."

We walked down a few doors and knocked on Violet's door. She opened the door and stood there.

"Good morning, Miss Conway," the man said.

"Good morning," Violet replied, looking straight ahead. "Mr. Furling will be pleased to see you both."

I looked at Violet. She didn't smile. We both looked straight ahead until the elevator doors opened.

Ahead of us was a table filled with fruits of all kinds, baked breads, and rolls. There was a buffet that was as long as you could see. I saw that there were four other people making the rounds around the buffet table.

"Welcome, Mr. Pinley and Miss Conway. Help yourselves to the breakfast feast. We will all meet here in this lobby in four hours. Enjoy." Mr. Furling walked away, accompanied by his bodyguards.

"You hungry, Violet?" I asked.

"Not really. Do you know what he has in mind, Ed?"

"No. What?" I picked up a plate and started for the biscuits and gravy.

"We are guinea pigs. He has a prototype of the device. He plans to try it using us as the first live subjects to be transported to another dimension. How can you eat at a time like this?" Violet asked.

"We will need the energy. Besides, we have a better chance to break his machine than anyone. If we get a chance to stop him, we've got to do it. I hope Zandra and Richard are out there looking for us," I said.

"They are, I'm sure. I hope they get here before this freak starts his experiment," she said.

"I noticed other people at the buffet," I said.

"I did too. I recognize two of them. Scientists, I believe. They worked at NASA in the past."

I finished the biscuits and gravy. It was great, but the art exhibit was even better. We spent a few hours walking through it.

All too soon, four hours were up, so we headed for the main lobby. There were four other people present. Someone gathered us up, and we headed into the conference room. We all took seats that were set in a row across the front of the large desk.

"Good day. I hope everyone had enough to eat, and I hope you all enjoyed the art exhibit. I want this experience to be memorable. Each one of you came here because of different reasons and circumstances. All of you have different interests in me or what I'm involved in. Some of you believe in me and what I want to do, because you believe you will become rich. And you might if you live," Himmler Furling said.

There was an awkward silence.

"Others planned to sabotage my work in order to cause failure. They planned to take my work after they caused it to fail and planned to reinvent it, hoping to claim it as their own. And those of you who are totally against me because of your moral beliefs, your idealisms? You were so against me that you even plotted to kill me. And all I want to do is be a pioneer in science." Himmler Furling looked at each person as he spoke.

"The information I received from Opus 8 is that Violet is a highbred human reptilian. She escaped from the Rufilian, a reptilian race that waged war in her dimension. Violet, you are the only person here to have traveled from one dimension to another. If you have the device, we don't need to test ours. It could save time and possibly lives," he said, grinning.

"I don't have it. I never had it. But, Mr. Furling, there is no need to sacrifice anyone to test your device. I have experience with traveling through dimensions. Let me explain. I was one of the first to enter the portal and live. That was over four hundred years ago, Mr. Furling, but I have not forgotten that moment of plunging myself into the blue light, not knowing my fate.

"After we started the device, the wall of light had started changing colors while we engaged the Rufilian who were chasing us. Some of our people panicked and ran into the light before it turned blue, and they perished. We held off the attacking group for as long as we could. I remember the shimmering light as it turned crystal blue. I closed my eyes and ran into it, and now I'm here. Mr. Furling, you may have the means by which I could return to my own dimension," Violet said.

"Four hundred years is a long time, Violet. Besides, our intelligence suggests that your highbred group has the device. You could have gone home anytime," Furling said.

"Someone like me could never have access to the device even if they had it," she replied.

"So if your people do not have the device, where is it?" he asked. "Lost or possibly hidden somewhere. If your scientist designed

a similar device, then I can be of some help with testing it. No one needs to die to see if it works. These past four hundred years, I have studied every discipline known to science and engineering. I can help you get the device paired with the energy grid and lead an expedition to another dimension. Once we reach the first dimension, we can set ordinances and begin mapping the first expedition. While there, you can get surface samples and determine if there are rare or precious metals. After all, you have two government scientists and two helpers," Violet said.

"Speak for yourself. I have no intentions of helping this madman," Mr. Smith said.

"You got that right. Now, Mr. Furling, we want our money back, and we demand you release us immediately. I intend to call my lawyers as soon as I get out of here," Walter Bright added.

Himmler Furling stood there, and the look on his face resembled a smashed grill on a 1959 Cadillac. His face was red, and the vein in his forehead seemed to swell.

"Mr. Smith, Walter Bright, it is unfortunate that you require so many things from me. You see, your money is just paper with dead presidents' faces printed on it, and you two are worthless excuses for human beings."

Himmler reached into his vest and pulled out a semi-automatic pistol. He fired two shots into the men's foreheads. They both fell and lay on the ground motionless.

"Now that this unpleasant little task is complete, is there anyone else who wishes to leave?"

No one spoke as Himmler walked around, playing with his pistol and twirling it in his hands.

"Good. That is good. Your proposition is interesting, Violet, but I must sleep on it. Everyone, please return to your rooms immediately."

Himmler's men rounded the remaining four of us up and accompanied us to our dorms.

Violet walked out, following Himmler's men. She didn't look at me as she left. The rest of us followed in silence. I wondered what she was up to. It didn't matter though; I trusted her with my life.

The next day, we gathered for breakfast. Violet nibbled on some rye toast.

"Are you serious about going home, Violet?" I asked.

She looked at me. "Yes, dead serious, Ed. I miss my own reality, my own dimension, my own people," she said.

"But you don't even know if any one of your kind survived all these years. It could be suicide for you if the Rufilian are still in power," I said.

"Then I will die. Maybe that's what should have happened to me instead of me being stuck here in your dimension. I'm tired of being a freak." Violet got up and walked away.

I remained seated as Himmler entered the room. Everyone stopped what they were doing and looked at him. Violet took a seat close to the front of the room.

"I trust everyone has rested up. I have considered Miss Conway's proposition and have decided to take her up on her offer. Miss Conway will accompany our team to the lab. The rest of you will be briefed on the equipment we will be using in the field. Depending on our progress, you could be called to participate at any moment, so be prepared. Meanwhile, you all have access to my personal library and gym, if you so desire." Furling smiled and walked away.

The conversation with Violet made no sense; she had never been this negative before. I assumed she was putting on a show for Himmler. After all, everything was being recorded. I decided to be watchful and quiet. I spent the afternoon in the library.

It was around 5:00 p.m. when Himmler Furling appeared.

Violet stood next to him.

"I have good news for everyone. Tomorrow we will begin at 6:00 a.m. sharp. Your gear will be issued in the morning. It promises to be a great day. Dinner is served," he said.

He walked out with Violet by his side. The rest of us walked behind them.

"Looks like you're on your own now," the man next to me said. "Yeah, I guess so. We just worked together. We weren't, you know"

"Yeah, I know. I have the same deal, except my partner is my ex-wife. At work, we make the best team. But at home, we fight like dogs and cats," he said.

"So you worked at NASA?" I asked.

"Yeah, that's where we met. Then we started a consulting firm. Shortly after that, we got divorced. Now we get along great. Our company is doing great. In fact, that's how we ended up here. By the way, I'm Leonard Gauthier. My ex-wife goes by Miss Leanne Rice. She kept her maiden name. I think she knew something I didn't," Leonard said with a smile.

"At least you both can share in the business," I said.

"Share, ha. I wish. She got 55 percent. I have 45 percent. Basically, I work for her," he said.

"Leonard, were you telling stories about me?" Leanne smiled and shook my hand.

"I'm Ed Pinley."

"It's a pleasure to meet you. I'm Leanne Rice."

"What do you mean that's how you both ended up here?" I asked.

"Himmler Furling had asked us to attend his speech in the VIP section. He sent a car for us. Needless to say, we never ended up at the speaking event. And just what is it you and Violet do?" Leonard asked.

"I'm Violet's assistant. I attend to the small stuff. She's the genius."

"It's good to know our place," he said. Leanne laughed.

Everyone sat down at their assigned seats. Violet's name had been removed from her spot at the table, and she was nowhere in sight. I watched as everyone talked to each other. I wondered what Violet had planned. We finished our meal and were served coffee. There was small conversation while we waited for Himmler Furling to speak.

"We have established a plan for our exploration into another dimension. Mr. Pinley, because of your bionic capabilities, we have chosen you to go first into whatever dimension we land in. You will wear a bracelet that will track you wherever you land. It will set us up to chart our journey, as well as keep track of your position. Mr. Pinley, I realize that you may end up in a very desirable place, and it may cross your mind to just disappear, in which case, I will shoot your girlfriend first, then each person held here every hour after that if you don't contact me or return," Furling said.

"What if something happens and I can't get back? Besides, you can't just kill all your scientists," I said.

"The tracking device you will wear is very advanced. It will be able to collect the information needed to come to that decision. If I need to kill everyone, I will, Mr. Pinley. There are plenty of suckers out there to take their place. Mr. Pinley, please report to the lab. That is all." He walked out of the room.

We made our way to the lab. Inside the lab, Furling paced for a few minutes, looking at his cell phone. I sat down and waited.

"Mr. Pinley, there are multiple reasons you're going first." He looked over at Violet, who was sitting behind her research table. "In case Miss Conway was going to kill me during our first round of traveling through dimensions, it would have been on this attempt. I hope she has everything dialed in."

Violet smiled at him as he walked by.

"All right, let's begin. Violet will describe the event that will occur," Furling said.

"In front of you, there will be a shower of light. When the energy grid and the device are paired, the light will change. It is important that you wait for the right color and vibration before you advance into the light. Once you're inside the light, continue to walk forward. The light will become weaker, and you will arrive in another place, another dimension. Do you understand, Ed?" Violet asked.

"Yes, I do."

"I will be in your earpiece. Follow my orders."

"What do I do if I encounter other beings or land somewhere inhabited?"

"That's where you'll have to play it by ear. If it is dangerous or violent, we can transfer you again to a different dimension. You have a mounted camera in your safety vest, and we will be monitoring conditions," she said. "Everyone, take your station. The pairing will begin in ten seconds."

I waited for the light show to begin. I was excited about going in first. I trusted that Violet had the device dialed in. We never talked about sensations, but I was having one. The hairs on my body stood up, and my skin crawled. I waited for the lights; it seemed like forever. I closed my eyes for what seemed just a moment and then opened them

84

again. I noticed a different shade of blue; it was shimmering. I could feel a vibration throughout my whole body.

"Ed, can you hear me? It's time to walk through the portal. Ed, it is time to walk through the portal."

A tiny voice in the back of my head told me to walk, and I did. I walked through the portal and opened my eyes to a very different world. I looked around. The ground appeared to be made up of sand and basalt. In the distance, the land appeared to be flat for miles. Behind me, there was a two-hundred-foot rock outcrop. Off to the north, there was a barren mountain range.

There was a cloud cover hovering around the base of the barren mountain. The cloud seemed very dense and was moving along quite mechanically. I activated the tracking device and waited for contact from Violet and Mr. Furling. I noticed the lights in the cloud's formation.

The lights resembled the flashing lightning we used to watch in the Midwest, where I grew up. This flashing lightning was different, more intense. It began to explode as it hit the ground. The cloud mass was moving toward my position. There was noise in my earpiece, then Violet's voice came through.

"Ed, can you hear me?"

"Yes, I'm fine. I seem to be alone here. There are no signs of life.

There is a storm of intense strength heading my way," I said. "Our readings indicate extreme electrical activity."

"I'm getting strong readings here as well. The storm is moving fast. I need to find cover or return," I said.

There was a flash of lighting and an explosion that knocked me off my feet. When I looked up, the portal was gone. I looked at the approaching storm and realized it was not a storm at all. Through the cloud cover, I could make out two humongous tube-shaped vessels that hovered above the ground. They must have been extracting minerals from the surface basically strip-mining. A series of lasers shot out of the craft, ripping the ground up in violent explosions. From a distance, it resembled lightning.

I looked off into the distance. I could see the path of destruction these machines had made. For as far as I could see, there was nothing but devastation. And now the machines were heading straight for me.

The lasers stopped, and the machines moved slowly. I looked around. I was trapped, standing at the bottom of a two-hundred-foot rock wall. All around me were smaller rock outcrops. I managed to crawl under a rock edge just as the machines passed over me. Then the two-hundred-foot rock wall opened up, and the vessels entered. I watched as they slowly made their way to a docking station.

I followed the vessels through the opening and entered the area. It resembled a large aircraft hangar. Behind me, the giant doors closed. I saw a ladder that led to a catwalk above the docking area. I climbed it and waited for the operators of the machines to exit. No one did.

I heard steps coming from the other direction and then saw five forms walking toward the machines. As they came closer, I could see that they were humans. I watched as they started their jobs.

They were controlling the equipment that was unloading the minerals the machines had collected. Everything seemed to be in powder form. There were various colored powders, probably every mineral known to mankind and whatever we don't know about.

I looked around. The people seemed to be alone in this docking area. I sat and watched. I could hear them speaking to one another; they were definitely American. I decided to make myself known. I climbed down the ladder and walked into the light. Everyone looked up. There was silence for some time.

"How did you get in here?" the closest man to me asked. His name tag read "Mac Johnston US Navy."

"I followed the machines in here and hid until I thought it was safe to make contact with you," I replied.

"You came from outside? We were told there were no life forms in this area," Mac said.

"Actually, there doesn't seem to be any life forms in this area. I came here from another dimension through a portal. How did you all get here? I see you're American Navy," I said.

"You came through a portal? Were you abducted? Did the Greys bring you here?" he asked.

"No, I came through a portal. I'm here on recon, you might say. My portal was knocked out by these machines, so I followed them inside here."

"We were all abducted, one way or another." Another man stepped up. "My name is Steve Ritter, US Air Force. There are various groups of aliens involved in abducting species from all over the universe. They use wormholes to travel from one dimension to another. The most commonly seen alien species are the Greys," he said.

"I have heard of the Greys. When were you abducted by them?" I asked.

"I was taken in 1941, in the Bermuda Triangle," Mac said.

"I was abducted in 1965, on a fishing vessel on Lake Michigan," another man said.

"My plane disappeared off the radar in 1973, over the Mojave Desert," Ritter said.

"You don't look over twenty-five years old. None of you look like you have aged," I said.

"You are right. We have not aged, and we are all healthy," Mac said.

"When the doors open for the machines to go out again, I can transport you all back home. I'll contact my people, and we can free you all. Our portal will transport you home," I said.

"This is our home. We have everything we need. We have wives, a home—everything we had when we were abducted, only better. If we went back to your dimension now, we would spend the rest of our lives being debriefed by our governments. We would not be free by any means. Our wives, our partners may just be holograms and our homes all an illusion, but I can say I'm happy. I'll be twenty-five years old until I'm terminated. I can live with that. I have a life. We all do. We do our job and go home and live the illusion that everyone back home does. Except we don't age, and life is always good," Mac said.

I was taken aback by his response, and everyone else in the group seemed to agree with him. They would rather stay here than rejoin the human race.

"I'll need to establish contact in order to return home. When will the doors open again?"

"We have concerns about your leaving. We don't want any unwanted visitors, if you know what I mean," Ritter said.

"My intentions are to leave here and never return. I won't tell them about you or this operation," I said.

"We can't take chances, sir. I'm afraid you can never leave," Mac said.

I didn't see it coming, but I definitely felt it, a four-fingered fist up against my forehead. I was seeing galaxies spinning around my head. Again, I was stuffing cotton back into my little stuffed animal's forehead, waiting for the lights to turn on. There was a polka band playing "Stairway to Heaven" in the background. I was relaxed now, very relaxed.

I don't know how long I was unconscious. When I finally opened my eyes, I was in a dark room, lying on the floor. I sat up. I felt a piece of paper stuck to my forehead. I peeled it off and read what was written.

> They are coming for you. You do not have much
> time. Outside the door, there is a ladder that leads to
> a maintenance catwalk. At the end of the walk, there
> is an outside filter access. From there, you can make

it outside. I believe I'm up for termination. Please come back for me. I'll be ready. Good luck. Jen.

I looked at the door; it was slightly ajar. I peeked out and saw the ladder. I climbed up to the catwalk. I heard some doors opening and the footsteps of what sounded like four or five individuals coming my way. I proceeded to the end of the catwalk and saw the filter door. I removed it and climbed inside. I closed the cover door and crawled toward the end of the tunnel. There was another door. I pushed it open and saw that I was on the side of a large cliff. Below me was a canyon nearly a hundred feet down. I wondered who had put the note on me, warning me that something or someone was coming for me. Their name was Jen. I had not seen a woman in that room.

"Ed, we have you. You've been off our tracking system for quite some time. Are you all right?" Violet's voice suddenly came through the earpiece.

"Violet, I'm okay. I lost the portal after that last lightning strike and had to seek cover," I replied.

"Mr. Pinley, your timing is excellent. Violet was about to eat a bullet if you hadn't shown up just now. In fact, she only had seven minutes left before I would have regrettably pulled the trigger," Mr. Furling said.

"That would have been your last mistake, Furling," I said.

"You're in no position to threaten me, Pinley."

"We don't have time for this, boys. Ed, are you ready? The portal is activated. It should appear in five seconds," Violet said.

"I'm ready."

Behind me, I could hear voices. Whoever was looking for me was coming my way. The blue light appeared before me, just a few feet off the cliff, in midair. It began to shimmer. The voices were getting closer. I looked below me. A hundred foot drop if I jumped too early, and certain capture if I didn't jump now.

I stepped back and leaped into the blue shimmering wall of light. I felt my body fall and began to scream, my arms waving above my head. My eyes were closed when I hit the floor of the laboratory. I heard laughing as I opened my eyes. Before me were four men aiming automatic weapons at me. Standing behind the armed men was Himmler Furling, who was holding a gun to Violet's head.

"Welcome back, Pinley. As you can see, I took some precautions for your return. Now I would hate to ruin this homecoming with yours or Violet's blood," he said.

"I won't be any trouble, Furling. You can call off the dogs," I said.

"I have studied the images that your body cam took. Pinley, you have discovered exactly what I was looking for. We have struck it rich the first time out. I like that. Miss Conway will lead the next expedition, along with me and my team. You will stay behind with the others." Himmler Furling grinned.

I looked around. There were four men in the room; all of them had a gun on me.

"The people inside are unarmed. They claim to have been abducted by aliens from our dimension years ago," I said.

"Don't worry about them. You have enough to worry about.

What else can you tell me about their operation?" Furling asked. "Once the machines dock, the workers come in and start the

unloading process. It looks like they have technology that turns minerals and precious metals into powder for easy transport. They place the powders in containers and then load the containers onto a platform. I don't know what happens to the containers after they are filled," I said.

"I'm sure we have the ability to figure that out. Mr. Reynolds will be at the controls. Mr. Pinley will be escorted to his cell."

I watched as one of the men who had previously had his gun aimed at me sat down at the control panel. There were no gauges or switches, just one button that read Engaged one way and Disengaged the other way.

Furling turned to Violet. I looked over at her. She avoided eye contact and spoke like she did not care about what was going to happen.

"As soon as we are outside the hangar, the tracking device will find us, Mr. Reynolds. I have preset the system to place us a mile west of where Ed was placed yesterday. In case they are looking for Mr. Pinley, we can observe the area before we enter. We plan to exit through the large bay doors," she said.

"How are you going to open the bay doors? The men there told me they are controlled by the Greys orbiting above the planet," I said. "I have built an explosive device that will blow the doors completely open," Violet replied.

"What about the workers inside?" I asked.

"They will need to seek cover when we activate the device. If they resist, we will have no choice but to eliminate them," she said.

I couldn't believe what she was saying. The look on my face must have pleased Furling.

"Good, Violet. I see you are on board," he said.

"Remember, Mr. Furling, after this run, I'm going home to my own dimension. I will do anything to make that happen, including killing you if you double-cross me. That's our deal," Violet said.

"As you wish, Miss Conway. But for now, you'll follow my orders until we complete this run. Is that clear?"

Violet avoided eye contact with me as Himmler's men led me away.

"Is that clear, Miss Conway?" Himmler Furling asked. "Yes, Mr. Furling, that is clear."

The two men led me away. The other one remained in the lab with Mr. Reynolds. We started walking. Both men held their guns on me as I walked in front of them. I noticed we were walking to an area I hadn't seen before.

"Where are we going?" I asked. "Shut up and keep walking."

We walked for a few more minutes. We entered what looked like a janitor's closet. There was a large drain in the floor and a hose for water on the wall.

"All right, Pinley, on your knees. You need a minute before I send you off to the afterlife?" one of the men asked.

I tried to think of something to say. Everything was happening so fast. Now here I was, kneeling in a janitor's closet, with a large gun resting its barrel on the back of my head.

"I guess I would like to pray if you don't mind," I said.

"Go ahead, Pinley. Pray all you want. You've got one minute." "Do you mind taking the gun off me while I pray? It's uncomfortable."

"I guess so. Frank, keep your gun on him." The man stepped back.

Just then, the lights went out. I did a leg sweep, knocking the executioner off his feet, his gun firing rapid shots as he fell to the ground. I looked at the other man. He was trying to see me in the dark. I was amazed that I could see perfectly. I hit the man, knocking him out. I picked up both guns. I heard footsteps coming toward me from down the hall. I stepped out of the janitor's closet, pulling the door shut and locking it behind me.

I heard more shouts and gunshots coming from the lab. I made my way toward the activity. I stopped behind a large pillar and looked into the lab. Zandra and Richard were looking at a screen on the wall. I looked around and saw that Furling's men were cuffed and lying face-first on the ground. The lights came back on; the power had been restored.

I walked into the room. The control screen came on. It showed Furling, Violet, and Furling's men walking toward the huge rock ledge overlooking the valley.

Behind the group was the two-hundred-foot rock wall containing the doors that the machines had entered through. Off to the right, a small door appeared. It opened.

"Oh no, don't go in!" I screamed.

I watched as the group entered the room, and then we lost contact. The screen went blank.

"They're inside! What about Violet? They will be caught by the Greys!" I looked over at Zandra and Richard.

"Ed, that was the mission. Furling is gone. Who knows what the Greys will do with him? Fitting sentence, if you know what I mean."

I couldn't believe what I was hearing. "What about Violet? She's one of us!"

I felt someone touch my arm, and I looked up. Violet stood in front of me.

"That was my hologram, Ed, but thanks for caring. I know she appreciates it." She smiled. I was relieved to see her.

"I could never leave you behind, Violet. I would go back for you. That's why it can't be over!" I exclaimed.

"What do you mean, Ed?" Zandra asked.

I took out the note I had found stuck to my forehead when I was held at the hangar, and I handed it to her.

"'They are coming for you. You do not have much time. Outside the door, there is a ladder that leads to a maintenance catwalk. At the end of the walk, there is an outside filter access. I believe I'm up for termination. Please come back for me. I'll be ready. Good luck. Jen,'" she read aloud.

"She saved my life. I'd like to return the favor. Violet, what about your hologram? Don't you want her back? And what about Furling?"

"What about Furling?"

"Do you really want that madman to be with a race of aliens that may want to exploit the human race? He is a genius, you know," I said.

Zandra smiled. "You have a point, Ed, but I think they killed everyone as soon as they entered the door."

"There is only one way to find out. Besides, they will not be expecting me, and I know a back way in," I said.

"You mean on that cliff?" Violet asked.

"Why not? The cliff is wide enough. If you put that portal exactly where it was before, I know I can jump it. You just need to have faith, that's all. The cliff will be there. I'll go in and get Jen, Violet's hologram, and anyone else who wants to leave, and be back on the ledge as soon as I can. When we make contact with you, we will be ready," I said.

"Count me in," Violet said, grabbing my hand.

"I wouldn't miss it for anything. Blindly jumping into the abyss!" Richard said.

"I can man the controls and get you all back safely. Excellent.

Let's do this." Zandra smiled. "Ed, you are special," she added. "I know. They told me that in grade school."

She kissed me on the cheek and stepped back. Taking command, she organized the mission.

"Ed will jump first. Once inside, he will find Jen and any others wishing to leave. Violet and Richard will enter ten minutes after Ed. They will try to locate and determine Himmler's fate. Eliminate him if needed. Ed, wait for the right conditions. Be ready in ten seconds. Are you set?" she asked.

"Yes."

I saw the lights shimmering and felt the vibration. I jumped, passing into and through the wall of light. I landed belly first on the cold stone ledge. I felt the wind grabbing at my body as I slid toward the ledge. I gripped the edge of a rock and held on as the wind pulled at me. Eight feet in front of me was the filter door. If I could reach the door, I could gain entrance into the hangar.

"Ed, can you hear me?" Violet's voice rang in my earpiece. "I'm on the ledge. The wind is too intense. Hurricane strength winds. Don't come," I said.

"Ed, are you all right?" I could hear the voice in my ear as I tried to crawl toward the filter door.

"Don't come. The wind is too strong."

I listened as they confirmed they would wait. I crawled, grabbing every edge or rock I could use as footing, and finally reached the door. It was two feet above my head. The wind was strong, and I was afraid I would be swept off the ledge if I reached up for the door.

Then the door swung open. I saw someone drop a rope out to me. It floated in midair just above my head. I grabbed it and began to climb toward the opening, the wind ripping at me and lifting me off the ledge. I was airborne, climbing toward the person at the other end of the rope. I reached the edge and pulled myself into the door opening. I lay on the floor exhausted, my eyes blurred.

"Quiet," the person leaning over me said.

I tried to focus, but my eyes were not adjusting to the light. I realized then that I was breathing hard.

"Terrible wind, that's what we call it. I hoped you would come before the winds came. I was afraid you would be blown away before I could reach you, and you almost did get swept away by gale-force winds," the woman said.

I still couldn't see well, but I could make out the person's shape.

The lady was small and petite. "Are you Jen?" I asked.

"Yes, I saw them bring you into my storage room after they hit you. Mac and the guys didn't know I was doing maintenance on the extracting lasers. I heard some noise and low talk. I crept closer and

95

heard them say they were going to contact the Greys and hand you over to them. They were afraid you would come back and cause trouble in their little paradise. They said you had a way out of here and that it had to be kept secret. No one was leaving. That was their deal with the Greys in exchange for the perfect fake life. That's when I snuck in and tried to wake you. I shook you, but you were not responding. I put that note on your forehead, hoping you would wake up in time and read it. I was hoping you would come back for me."

"How did you know I was here?"

"I put a transmitter on you. It's in your pocket. It's small." I reached in and found it.

"When you arrived outside, I was waiting here when it went off," Jen said.

"Where are Mac and the boys?" I asked.

"They are in the hangar. There was some activity, so I took advantage of it and slipped away up here."

"Do you know what activity there was?" I asked.

"The Greys arrived. I know that I heard them docking." "How long before they know you're missing?"

"I don't know. I'm only maintenance. I'm not allowed in the docking area. They don't pay a lot of attention to me most of the time," she said.

"Are there any others wanting to leave here?"

"No, they are all happy with their fake lives here. They are of the upper class. Their engineering talents are needed by the Greys, so they are provided with the perfect life. Less talented maintenance people have good lives just as fake as theirs, just not as perfect. I'm the last maintenance person left on this project. When I'm done here, I'll either be transferred to another mining camp like this one or terminated. I would rather take my chances going back with you."

I looked at Jen. She appeared to be in her late twenties. She had a name tag: "Jennifer Higgins, US Navy." "When were you abducted?" I asked.

"The year 1959. I was on a coast guard vessel on Lake Michigan. We were searching for a vessel in distress. There was fog, and then a storm blew in. Before we knew it, our ship was in distress. We were taking in water, tilting to one side.

"There was a weird light surrounding us. I felt strange, like I was being lifted off the ground. When I woke up, I was looking into the eyes of an alien, a Grey. An American pilot was in the room. He helped me adjust to my surroundings and became my mentor. He trained me to perform the maintenance on the lasers. He said it would save my life and keep me out of the mines. He was right. I've been doing maintenance ever since I was abducted. I don't count the years," she said.

I handed her my helmet. "Here, put this helmet on. There is a mic inside. You will be in contact with the people I'm with. Can you tie yourself off in here and go out the door far enough to get reception?"

"Yes, I can do it."

"Tell them that you are Jen, that Ed went in to find out the condition of Mr. Furling. Tell them not to come, because the wind is too strong. Tell them you will notify them as soon as the wind dies down," I said.

I hoped they could receive our signal. I made my way toward the docking station. That was where Mr. Furling, Violet's hologram, and the team walked in. As I got closer, I saw Mac and the same men I had seen on my trip here earlier. They were gathered in a circle around Mr. Furling. Out of Mr. Furling's sight, off to one side stood three Greys. I was amazed at their small size.

"Please listen to me. I can make you all rich beyond your dreams. I can take you all away from here, where you will be kings. You'll never have to answer to the aliens ever again. Think of that!" Furling said, smiling.

"Sir, if we let you go, others will come just as you have. You don't understand that what you are offering is worthless to us. We have perfect lives, with perfect wives and partners. We never suffer from any illness or problems. What you're offering sounds like hell to me and the rest of us. Too much wealth is a cancer. It will eat you alive. You always want too much, don't you, sir? That is why we cannot believe that what you tell us is true. Your greed makes you dangerous and a liar. We are sorry for the actions we are forced to take here today. You and your group must never leave here," Mac said.

I looked around and saw Violet's hologram tied up and sitting in another room. Furling's men were facedown; they looked unconscious. I made my way toward a ladder that brought me down to their level. I heard Furling arguing.

"What are you saying? I can't stay here for the rest of my life! I'm an adventurer, a pioneer! I am probably the most powerful man in the world! I will pay you whatever you require for my safe return to my dimension. Tell the Greys I can offer them any dimension or world they want. It's all at my fingertips!" He was yelling louder with every sentence.

"What about your men and the girl?" Mac asked. "You can have them. It's part of the deal," Furling said.

"That's what we thought you would say, Mr. Furling," Ritter said. I was five feet from Violet's hologram. I crawled until I could reach her ties. I cut them. The hologram remained still as she listened to Mr. Furling try to buy his way out of here.

"I'm offering you the deal of a lifetime! You can have whatever you want! You do realize that!" Furling pleaded.

"Mr. Furling, we have that deal right now. Anything we desire, we can have. Any pleasure, any adventure, anything our hearts may desire, we can have. Now we know you're a businessman, so we have prepared an offer for you. The Greys acknowledge that you are talented and gifted. They would hate to see such talent wasted in the mines," Mac said.

"Good. So they've been thinking about what I've been saying, and now they have an offer?" Furling sounded excited.

"Yes, sir," Ritter said.

Violet and I crawled slowly toward the ladder and made our way up to the catwalk.

"Well, go ahead. I'm anxious to hear it," Furling said.

"We have a position in the maintenance department, laser technician. You can start immediately. We have someone who can train you," Mac said.

There was a silence that came over the room. Violet and I had to stop crawling toward the door and remain still to avoid being heard.

"Well, Mr. Furling, are you excited to join us?" Mac asked. "I'm speechless and shocked that you would even ask me to join you. You all are a pathetic group of nobodies in a nowhere land, living a fantasy. Nothing is real. Your hologram wives, your fancy cars—all fake!" Furling said.

I stopped to listen.

"Well put, Mr. Furling. You're right, but what you don't understand is, your world is just as fake. You pretend that the people around you like you, that your life is fulfilled with good fortune, that happiness abounds. All the time, you wallow in your wealth. You start becoming sick from it. Your wealth starts to eat you alive. Your soul suffers. People wait for you to die. We, on the other hand, do not age. We don't thirst for great wealth. We have all that we need, never in excess," Mac said.

I heard the men begin to walk off, leaving Furling and Mac alone.

"Where are you all going? What about negotiations?" Furling asked.

"They are over, Mr. Furling. You and your people will be leaving with the Greys," Mac replied.

The Greys pointed a small stick at Furling and his men. They instantly became suspended in midair. They seemed to be in a trance as they floated away.

"Mr. Ritter, where is the girl?" Mac asked.

"We have her in the back, tied up. I'll get her," Ritter said. "Get her. The Greys have a particular interest in her. They say she is not human," Mac said.

I started down the catwalk. Violet's hologram was just ahead of me. She stopped and looked back. We heard the men searching for her in the rooms down the hall below us. I opened the door, and we crawled toward Jen.

"How is the wind?" I asked.

"The wind is gusting at about thirty-five to forty miles per hour. It's tough, but we can get on the ledge. Your people are waiting for us," Jen said.

We heard Mac and his men begin to search the area directly below us.

"Okay, let's go."

Jen, Violet's hologram, and I all stepped onto the ledge.

"Ed, I have you. Are you all ready? The wall of light will appear in five seconds," Zandra said through the earpiece.

Mac and his men were running toward us, twenty feet away.

The blue light began to shimmer; we could feel the vibration. "Ready. All right, Jen, don't jump till Violet does," I said. "Jump into midair? Are you crazy?"

Violet's hologram grabbed Jen and jumped. Behind me, I could hear the group approaching. I hesitated for a moment to look back.

Then I stepped back and jumped. The wall of light disappeared before me. I started to descend toward the canyon a hundred feet below me.

*****

"Where is Ed?"

Zandra and Richard stood drenched in fire retardant. Violet looked at Jen and her hologram.

"He was coming right after us," her hologram said.

Zandra looked at the tracking screen. "He seems to be floating in midair. Now he's gone," she said.

"What? Gone? What do you mean by that?" Violet asked.

"He must have been captured. If he missed the wall of light, he would have plunged to his death, and it would show us where he had fallen," Zandra explained.

The fire alarms were blaring in the background. Opus 8 had almost completely cut through the metal doors. There was little time left.

"Chester, engage the unit now." Richard talked into his phone as he helped Jen up off the floor. "We are almost out of here. As soon as the portal opens," he said.

"What about Ed?" Violet asked.

"We're out of time, Violet. We need to go now."

The wall of light appeared. Violet, her hologram, Jen, Richard, and Zandra walked into the light just as Agents Henderson and Frost entered the room.

*****

I was standing, looking down into the large eyes of a Grey. Its oversized head and small body made it look like the little thing was

101

about to tip over at any given second. Mac entered the room and closed the door.

"You came back. That's exactly what we didn't want to happen," he said.

"You could have let me fall to my death, and that would have solved the problem," I replied.

"Yes, but our friend here has interest in you and the woman," he said.

"Jen?"

"No, not Jen. She was scheduled for termination after this assignment. The fact that she is gone satisfies the Greys. We are talking about the woman who came here with Mr. Furling."

I knew he was talking about Violet's hologram. "She is not here, Mac."

"We know that," Mac said.

"She is not coming back. No one else is coming back. Our mission is complete. They probably think I'm dead," I said.

"What was your mission?" he asked.

"Mr. Furling had been flagged by our intelligence as a possible threat to life everywhere. As he was an extremely intelligent but seriously dangerous person with psychotic tendencies, we were to eliminate him. We did not want to kill him. We thought we could place him somewhere in the universe where he couldn't hurt anyone else, somewhere he couldn't use his intelligence to inflict his will on others, somewhere the only person he could hurt was himself."

The Grey seemed amused by my comment. I saw a little movement in its eyes.

"Very amusing, Mr. Pinley. That was the reason we have forced some of our bad seeds to your earth. They lived among your civilization, so I do understand. Your bad seed, Mr. Furling, is mild compared to some of the entities we have placed on your earth in the past. But be assured that Mr. Furling and his men will be put to work in the mines until we decide to terminate them."

I was hearing the Grey's voice in my head. It was communicating with me telepathically.

"The woman with you was not human, and you have multiple DNA readings, implants, bionic arms and legs. Neither of you are just human. That was why I had interest in you both. I needed to know if you were a threat to us." The Grey looked at me.

"I came back because of Jen, the laser maintenance person. I also wanted to retrieve Violet's hologram and be sure Mr. Furling was taken care of," I said.

The Grey looked into my eyes. Its eyes were larger. I noticed there were no eyelids; it never blinked. I can't say how long I looked into its eyes.

"I believe you, Mr. Pinley. You will be going home soon." The Grey looked at Mac and then walked away with two other Greys.

"Mr. Pinley, I don't have to tell you how lucky you are. You must be a very good person. I've never seen anyone released before. When that Grey looked into your eyes, he read you—your energy, your essence. Most humans end up in the mining camps or working in the technical fields. You are being transported back to earth, your own dimension. Come with me. You will need to get ready for the travel," Mac said.

I followed him into a room that had a full-body chair.

"That is your seat. You'll be in suspended animation until you arrive back on earth. Then they will place you somewhere in or around your home," he said.

"How do they know where that is?" I asked.

"They know everything about you now, Mr. Pinley."

Mac left the room. I sat down on the chair, then lay back, noticing how comfortable I was. I closed my eyes and thought of that moment I thought I was going to fall to my death. Time seemed to stand still. Then I just floated there until the Greys brought me back inside.

"Ed, Ed, wake up."

I opened my eyes. Zandra, Violet, Violet's hologram, Richard, Jen, and Chester were all looking at me. I was lying on the couch in my apartment.

"You're alive!" Violet grabbed me and hugged me.

"We thought you were dead or captured," Zandra said.

"I've been here the whole time, Mr. Pinley. I never heard you come in," Chester added.

"We just got here through the portal in the safe room moments ago," Richard said.

Jen just looked at me, wide-eyed.

"How long have you been here?" Zandra asked.

I was looking at a room of very confused people. For once, I was the only one who knew anything. I decided to savor the moment.

"I'll have to explain later. I'm exhausted." I closed my eyes and drifted off to sleep.

*****

I opened my eyes to a wonderfully sunlit room my room. I got up off the couch I had fallen asleep on and walked into the kitchen. I watched as Violet finished drying some dishes. I was about to speak, when someone touched my face. I turned and looked to see that it was Violet.

"Are you the hologram, or is she?" I pointed to the other Violet at the counter.

"I'm for real, the real Violet." "Good. I have a request," I said. "What is it, Ed?"

"Shift into the real you your hybrid human look, your natural state. You looked beautiful when you were shifting back and forth at the Squat and Gobble. I love your eyes. I want you to be just as you are," I said.

Violet smiled and became herself. In her natural state, she stood over eight feet tall, her muscular body covered with different colors. Her skin was like human skin, her features slightly larger than a human's. Her eyes were larger, dark, with hints of red and green. She had white pupils. Violet didn't hold back; she was totally in her natural state. She was beautiful.

"You look beautiful, Violet," I said.

"You like me this way, Ed? I was told to never reveal the real me to you. They thought you would, you know, not like me unless I was in my human form," she said.

"Well, whoever thought that was wrong. I like you for you. In your natural state, you are stunning and incredibly beautiful," I said.

Violet bent down, picked me up, and kissed me like I'd never been kissed before. She gently put me down. "Thank you, Ed. That means a lot." She smiled.

There were footsteps coming up my stairs. The door opened, and Chester and Jen walked in. Jen looked excited; she had her arms filled with bags. I looked over at Violet. She had already changed back into her human form.

"I went shopping with Chester. He thought I needed to have modern clothes," Jen said, smiling.

"Hello, Mr. Pinley. I trust you slept well on your couch?" Chester asked.

"I did. I feel refreshed," I said.

"Good. Then you can fill us in on what happened to you." Richard had walked in from the back room. "Zandra will be right out," he added.

"I've got fresh coffee for everyone," Violet said. She looked over at her hologram as Zandra entered the room.

"I've got some great gossip for you all" Violet's hologram suddenly burst into a cloud of fading light specks.

"She needs to charge. She's babbling again. Go ahead, Ed. I'm ready," Violet said as she sat down across from me at the table.

Zandra smiled and took a seat next to Richard. And I began.

I told them of my encounter with the Greys. Afterward, Zandra announced that the team would be heading back to their base. Jen would accompany them back as well.

"Mr. Pinley, you and I will be heading off for a few book signings, and then there is the UFO conference. By the way, I booked you a music gig too," Chester said triumphantly.

"Music gig?" I asked.

"They need a drummer for the conference band. It's a group of trombone players and accordions thirty-five, to be exact. They had a drum machine, but they said it speeds up or slows down. So they want you to drum for them. It will be so exciting, sir," he said.

Everyone in the room had a straight face. I was afraid Chester was serious.

Chapter 8

Body Bag

Steve Mann slowly walked toward the last bus that had been waiting to leave the research center. It was New Year's Eve, and he had regrettably just finished his shift. It was more than a two-hour bus ride to his car, located in the last parking lot outside of Sand Draw, Wyoming. He usually enjoyed working late, especially during the holidays. His work was fun. It really was all he had left.

But today, Steve had witnessed something he would never forget. He knew that what he had witnessed would change his life forever. He tried to squeeze the images out of his head, but he could not.

Steve's job was on Opus 8's reverse-engineering team. They had just completed the propulsion system for an alien spacecraft believed to have been piloted by aliens known as Greys. Opus 8 had brought in a captured Grey pilot to activate the craft's propulsion system. Steve hoped his reaction to that event had gone undetected. There were always watchers in every research team. The wrong reaction could cost you your job.

He hated New Year's Eve, along with Halloween, St. Patrick's Day, and Christmas. One year ago, he had arrived home to an empty house and a note written in red ink. His wife and his joint bank account had disappeared, along with their Land Rover. He could still see the two words his wife had scribbled down on the back of a peeled-off label

107

from a Corona beer bottle: Good luck. He tried to think of something else as he entered the bus.

"Good evening, Mr. Mann," the bus driver greeted Steve in his monotone voice. Irritated with Steve's slowness, he stared straight ahead.

"Good evening, Dan. Thanks for waiting." "No problem. It's my job, sir," Dan replied.

Steve walked to the back of the bus even though he was the only one on it. He sat down. Again, the images of that day invaded his mind. He closed his eyes, trying to erase it, trying to forget what he had witnessed what he had become part of.

He had hoped he would fall asleep during the long ride to the parking lot. But the images kept haunting him, and now he was becoming paranoid. He feared he had blown it.

One week ago, his best friend, Tomas Hinter, had reacted similarly. The next day, he was offered a desk job in Virginia, or he could choose to retire early. Anyone discharged from the team was forbidden to have contact with current team members. So Tomas had disappeared, leaving no forwarding address. The official government memo about Tomas said that he had led a successful career with the Air Force and that he was looking forward to moving back to the Midwest to enjoy his early retirement.

Steve, desiring to keep his job, did not try to contact him after he had left the team. Tomas never contacted Steve, out of professional courtesy. Tomas and Steve had known each other since kindergarten. They had graduated from the same high school and had gone to college together. They had both served in the Air Force and finally ended up working together on the same secret project for Opus 8.

Steve's mind drifted off to what he had witnessed, what had been done in the name of research. He knew it was wrong, probably sinful. He tried in vain to push the incident out of his head.

"Mr. Mann, we are here," Dan said.

Steve opened his eyes. He had not heard the bus stop. The interior lights seemed brighter than normal. "Thanks, Dan."

He exited the bus. He stared at his car as the bus drove away. He walked toward his car, wondering what the outcome would be on Monday when he returned to work. Had the watchers in the operations room seen his reaction, or did he successfully cover it up?

He leaned against his car. He really had nowhere to go. His home had little welcoming for him. He hadn't replaced the furniture since his wife took everything one year ago. He slept on a camping mat with a sleeping bag on his bedroom floor. He rarely cooked anything, even though he still had several pans his wife had left behind in the cupboard. Ramen noodles with freeze-dried shrimp would be this year's New Year's Eve feast.

Off in the distance, Steve could hear a vehicle approaching. This was strange; there were never any vehicles out here this time of night. He had heard that there had been some break-ins during the Christmas holidays. The official memo advised against leaving vehicles in the parking lot during the holidays. Perhaps whoever was coming up the hill were the same people who had broken into vehicles during Christmas.

Steve fished for his keys. He thought they were in his jacket, but he could not find them. He looked up and saw the headlights coming up the hill toward the parking lot. He reached into his pants pocket. Finally, he found the keys.

The vehicle was now less than two minutes away. He couldn't start his car now and try to leave. If they were thieves or carjackers, they would block his exit, drag him out of his car, and probably kill him. There had been incidents with some of the locals involving vandalism and some fights. Basically, the locals did not like outsiders from Washington, DC.

The parking lot was empty and very large. There was no place to hide. Steve looked at his keys. He pushed the trunk button. The trunk opened. He looked inside and saw that there was a latch he could pull to get out after the oncoming vehicle left. He crawled in and pulled the trunk down, letting it close completely. He waited and listened as the car came to a stop.

He moved slightly, just enough to view the two men through the small hole in his trunk. The men approached his car immediately. They examined the car, looking inside and finding no one. Steve wondered who these men were. They were not security, and they didn't look like carjackers. He pondered whether he should just get out and explain to these men what had just happened. They were probably researchers just like him. But he waited and listened to their conversation.

"Looks like somebody left their car. Run the plate. Find out who it is," one of the men said. The man seemed distracted and angry. "Where are they? They should have been here by now," he added.

Both men stood just a few feet from Steve's car, texting on their cell phones.

"Looks like Dr. Wilson has been taken care of. Now all we need to do is find Hinter, and bada bing, bada boom, Hinter will be history," the man said.

Steve listened. As the men talked, he realized Tomas Hinter was in danger.

"This car belongs to Steve Mann. You are right. He is a research engineer," the second man said.

"I wonder why he left his car parked here." The man walked closer and looked into the passenger side again. "He probably had car trouble. If he leaves the car here too long, it will be stripped down and hauled off," he said, laughing.

"Yeah, it's almost as bad as New York City, and we're in the boonies. Should I get the bag ready, Henderson?" the second man asked.

"Yeah, grab that bag and bring that thing here," Henderson said. The man opened the back door of their car and grabbed a large black bag. He carried the black bag over and placed it on the ground

in front of Henderson.

"Thanks, Frost. I guess now we wait," Henderson said.

Steve saw the large black bag. He recognized it immediately. Fear now ran through his whole body. He realized who they were. He also knew that if they found him, he was a dead man. It was bad enough that they had identified him.

What he was witnessing didn't make sense to him. Those men were holding the body bag that contained the body of a Grey. He remembered watching the Grey's body being loaded into that very bag.

"I think I hear them coming," Frost said.

Steve watched as a black SUV pulled up to the two men standing in the parking lot. The SUV's back window lowered. It was too dark for Steve to see the man inside the vehicle.

"Good evening, Senator Dawson," Henderson said.

"Do you have the proof for me, gentlemen? Or have I wasted my time again on New Year's Eve?" Senator Dawson asked.

"Senator, we have what you requested. Do you have what we need?"

"Agent Henderson, do you really think I would carry all that money here in the dead of night on New Year's Eve?" The senator looked at Steve Mann's car. "Why is there a third car here, Agent Henderson?"

"We checked it out. No one in it. Most likely, they had car problems and left it here. It is New Year's Eve, Senator. Hard to get a tow perhaps," Agent Henderson said.

"I'm well aware of what day it is, Agent Henderson. We will meet again after my scientists examine the contents and decide if it's real."

"Senator, we took a big chance on securing this body. I assure you it's real." Agent Henderson then loaded the body bag into the back of the SUV.

"Good to hear that, gentlemen. I'll need till tomorrow morning to confirm the contents. I will return the alien's body then. That should give you enough time to put the body bag back by Monday," Senator Dawson said.

"All right, Senator. You have my personal number. We will be waiting for your call. Have the money there this time," Henderson said.

"You sound confident, Henderson. I like that. If it is what you say it is, I'll have the money ready when you arrive tomorrow morning."

The window rolled up, and the black SUV drove away. "I hate that bastard," Agent Frost said.

"Yeah, I know. I don't trust him at all. I'll be happy when he returns the body and we can put it back in the research lab," Agent Henderson said.

"What if he doesn't pay us?" Frost asked.

"He will pay, one way or another. Let's get out of here. He will be calling us in a few hours," Henderson said.

Steve watched as the two agents drove away. He waited until he could no longer hear the sound of the vehicle. Slowly, he raised the trunk open. He looked out at the parking lot. It was empty and silent. He climbed out of the trunk and stood there, looking at the night sky. He realized he could never go home again, and he could never go back to work. Steve needed to find Tomas Hinter. He had a good idea where to look. He threw his car keys and his cell phone into the front seat of his car and walked away. Before he could find Tomas Hinter, Steve needed to become a ghost, someone who disappears.

Chapter 9

The Clown and I

Chester and I returned from the book tour. The actual concert with the accordions and trombones went well at the UFO conference. We played "Stairway to Heaven." Everything went smoothly. After arriving home, I spent a few days at the club, jamming with a local jazz group. Meanwhile, Chester was getting ready for another book tour coming up in a month.

"Mr. Pinley, there is a letter for you," Chester said. "Thanks, Chester. I'll read it after my workout."

"There seems to be some urgency, sir." He placed the letter on the desk. "Zandra and Richard will be arriving soon. They requested that you read the letter as soon as possible."

Chester left the room. I picked the letter up and read it. It had been written using words cut out of magazines and newspapers.

> Opus 8 is killing Greys. I have seen it with my own eyes. I am afraid for my life because of what I have seen. I believe somebody wants me dead. I have not gone home or anywhere people may know me. I have no phone, so if you want to take my case, meet me tomorrow morning in the pedestrian mall downtown during the farmers' market. I will know who you are, and I will come to you.

An hour later, Zandra and Richard sat at the table. They were analyzing the note. Finally, Richard picked it up.

"The note is not signed. There are two people in question who could be looking for Ed at the farmers' market. They are Tomas Hinter and Steve Mann. Tomas Hinter was released from the team over a week ago. He never picked his car up. He hasn't been heard from since that day. Steve Mann never returned to work. He disappeared on New Year's Eve. They found his car abandoned in the parking lot," he said.

"What do we know about these guys?" I asked.

"Opus 8 knows everything about them. They recruited both men into their research project. When someone is recruited by Opus 8, that recruit's common public information becomes top secret and disappears. The recruits keep their name, that's all. During the last few years, Opus 8 has recruited scientists right out of the military branches. Some of the recruits did not know they were joining Opus 8. They believed they were still in some branch of the Air Force, doing research for the Air Force. So far, three of last year's recruits have left the research team. Two of them remain missing. The third one, Dr. Wilson, was killed in a freak car accident yesterday. Dr. Wilson had been discharged from the medical team the day before," Zandra said.

"Tomas Hinter and Steve Mann neither of them have been seen since they left the research center. Neither one ever went home. Both abandoned their cars and cell phones. They both disappeared without a trace," Richard said.

"I wonder which one of these two people this guy will turn out to be," I said.

"Hinter was discharged about a week ago. Steve Mann never returned to work after the New Year's Eve holiday. They found his car still parked at the parking lot. Someone had stripped it down. They took all the tires and broke all the windows. The difference between Mr. Hinter and Mr. Mann is that Mr. Mann had not been discharged from the research team. Mr. Hinter had been discharged. I bet tomorrow's guy will be Mr. Mann. I think they got to Hinter just like they got to Dr. Wilson. We just haven't found Hinter's body. Maybe we never will," Zandra said.

"I think it's going to be Mr. Hinter. I bet Opus 8 got to Mr. Mann before his official notice was delivered. Something must have occurred that he witnessed that made it necessary for him to disappear immediately," Richard countered.

"All right, let's get some sleep. We hit it at 4:00 a.m. Chester will go first and survey the area. Richard and I will be strolling the streets, blending in. The farmers' market people arrive at 5:00 a.m. Ed, what time do you normally head down to the farmers' market?" Zandra asked.

"About six or six thirty. I grab a coffee at Louie's, and I meander to the market," I said.

"Good. Do the same as you always do. Opus 8 has been watching you for months, so they will recognize anything you do that's out of character. Try to act normal. We will have you in sight at all times. You are wired, so we will hear everything going on around you," she said.

The next morning, I walked slowly, trying not to look around too much. I stopped and talked with the bread lady and bought my cinnamon raisin roll. I watched as the children's parade began. It included leashed dogs dressed up in costumes. There were painted faces on the children and clowns walking on stilts. There seemed to be more clowns walking around on stilts than usual.

I looked around to locate anybody I knew. There were the regulars who always attended. They gathered around the breakfast burrito stand; the line was long. Soon more people were sitting in chairs and at the picnic tables where I always sat. There were more people than usual, but this was the last farmers' market for the season. People from all over the area came for the last one.

I ate my cinnamon roll with whipped butter and enjoyed a cup of Louie's cold brew coffee. The clowns were throwing candy out to the kids who were standing on the roadside as they passed. One of the clowns on stilts stopped and looked down at me.

"Are you Mr. Pinley?" the clown asked, their voice soft. I looked up at the clown. I could not hear clearly what was being said.

"Don't move in yet, Richard. According to the note, the person should know Ed," Zandra said into Richard's earpiece.

"Copy that. Have you heard anything from Chester?" he asked. "No," Zandra replied.

"Excuse me, sir. Are you Mr. Pinley?" the clown asked again. I nodded.

The clown reached into their shoulder bag, pulled out an envelope, and started to hand it to me.

All of a sudden, everyone around me and the clown grabbed the both of us. They pulled the clown down from the stilts and dragged the clown into the alley directly behind us. Other people dragged me into the same alley. I quickly realized it was not Zandra and Richard who had executed this grab. A man in a suit approached me. I recognized him.

"Mr. Pinley, it's nice to see you again," Agent Henderson said. He was holding the envelope the clown had tried to give me. I could hear the clown, whom they had pinned against the wall.

"What is wrong with you people? Let go of me!" the clown was screaming.

"Excuse me, Mr. Pinley. I'll be right back," Agent Henderson said. He walked over to the enraged clown. "Frost, please remove that disguise from this piece of shit. Let's see which one it is."

Frost reached over and tried to remove the wig and oversized nose. The clown kicked out at him, barely missing his crotch. He put his fist into the clown's face. The clown went limp. Frost removed the disguise. Behind the oversized nose and bright-red hair was a young woman who was maybe twenty.

"Shit. Take her to the van," Henderson said.

He walked over to me and glared at me for a few seconds. He was holding the envelope in his hand. He opened it and pulled out a card and showed it to me. It was blank.

"Pinley, somehow you have something to do with this. I should take you in right now." Agent Henderson was very angry. I expected a fist in the face any second.

Behind us, toward the back of the alley, there was an old woman in a wheelchair trying, without success, to climb up her ramp into the back of her van. We both turned to see what was going on.

Henderson looked back at me. "You want to help her, Pinley? Be my guest. Make yourself useful. I don't have time for this." He turned and walked away.

The rest of the people who had grabbed the clown and me were all gone. I looked over at the old woman. She was still trying to get her wheelchair up her ramp and into her van.

"Excuse me, ma'am. Can I help you?" I asked.

"I can do it, sonny." The old woman made another attempt to enter the van and rolled back onto the street.

"Let me help you." I grabbed her wheelchair and slowly pushed her up and into the van.

"Thank you very much, sonny. Can you push me all the way in?

I need to secure my wheelchair," the old woman requested.

I pushed her toward the front. Suddenly, the van doors closed behind me. I felt a sting on my arm, and everything went dark.

*****

"Richard, have you located Ed or the clown?" Zandra asked. "Henderson and Frost have the clown in their vehicle. The clown appears to be a woman. I don't see Ed anywhere," Richard replied.

"I don't know where Chester is either," Zandra said.

"Chester here. Sorry I missed everything. I was following some suspicious people when the local police needed to talk to me," Chester said.

"What do you mean, Chester?" Richard asked.

"I'm positive I recognized a couple of the spectators. I believe they are with Opus 8. I tried to follow them, when the police came and detained me for a while," Chester replied.

"They must have been the group that grabbed Ed and that clown," Richard said.

Chapter 10

Alien Rescue

"**M**r. Pinley, can you see the light?"

I recognized the voice. It came from inside my head. It was familiar.

"Mr. Pinley, the light. Can you see it?" the voice asked again. "Yes, I see a faint yellow light." I communicated without speaking.

"Mr. Pinley, try to open your eyes. You are still seeing through your mind."

Next to me stood the Grey that had saved my life and put Furling and his men in the mines. That was the familiar voice inside my head.

I could feel my eyes starting to open. I peeled back my eyelids; it felt like I was peeling an orange. The light was intense, almost hurtful. I slowly focused on it. I was heading toward it, just above the tree line.

We floated toward a rocky ridge, looking down at the research center's entrance. I was on a Grey flying saucer. Below us, nestled between three large stone outcrops, sat the research center operated by Opus 8. It was hidden from view unless you flew directly over it. There was one road leading into it, with four guards at the entrance and a number of guards around the compound. There was an employee bus that arrived and dropped off the employees at the main entrance inside the compound.

"Mr. Pinley, the research center is below us. They cannot see us. We are using a cloaking device. There are two smaller buildings next to each other. The building to the west is where our pilots and medical team are being held. Across from that building is the hangar. That is where our spacecraft is being reverse-engineered. They have already killed one of our kind in the name of science your science," the voice said.

There was an uncomfortable silence.

"Why did one of your kind die in there?" I asked.

"The researchers have managed to reverse-engineer one of our more advanced spacecraft that they had recovered. The spacecraft did not crash, so it is in perfect condition. They captured the medical team and crew that were on board. The craft set down in a spot we had used earlier in our exploration. The crew landed safely, and the medical team exited to collect samples. They were in the jungle, somewhere in a place you call Peru. They were hunting for herbs that can only be found in that region. After everyone had exited the craft, as they were preparing to start their assignment, they were surrounded by heavily armed soldiers. The crew and medical team surrendered without incident and were taken away. Opus 8 retrieved the spacecraft and brought it here. We've had the spacecraft under observation.

"We are running out of time, Mr. Pinley. If the research team gets the ship fully operational, they will have access to a multidimensional portal device similar to the one you and your group used. During the researchers' attempt to start the final stage, they tried to force one of the Grey pilots to activate it by placing the pilot's hand in the activation portal. There was a scuffle. The researchers ended up sedating the pilot to make him more cooperative. When they put the pilot's hand in the activation portal, the sedation had kicked in, and the portal wouldn't work. That was a little over a week ago in your timescale.

"The next time, they tried to force one of our pilots to start up the craft. The pilot refused. They cut his hand off and left him on the floor, bleeding to death. Their doctors couldn't save him. They didn't know what to do with a Grey. The pilot died before they could activate the final stage. That was a few days ago.

"We are running out of time, Mr. Pinley. If the humans are successful in starting stage three, we will have no other choice but to destroy the compound and everything in it. There will be military engagement in which humans would not survive. It is crucial that the humans do not gain access to the technology inside the Grey spacecraft," the Grey said.

I felt the burden the Grey was carrying. There was a deep sadness, perhaps anger of some sort, and the desire for a positive outcome. And now the alien had to enlist the help of a human.

"Mr. Pinley, we are counting on you," the Grey said. I looked into its eyes.

That was the last thing I could remember. Off in the distance, I could hear voices. They were coming from outside of my head. They were the voices of Zandra and Richard.

"Let's pour water on him," Zandra said. "Ed, open your eyes," Richard said.

"Look at this, Richard." She opened up a folded newspaper. The headline read "Senator Dawson and bodyguard still missing since New Year's Eve. No trace of foul play. The senator's car was found still running on New Year's night on County Road 215. There is a massive multicounty search underway." Zandra read the headline out loud.

I opened my eyes. Everything was still blurry, but I could make out the shapes of my two friends staring down at me. When I was able to focus, I noticed I was sitting in an oversized leather chair. There were pictures hanging on the wall that showed cowboys roping steers and Indians in their tepees, smoke rising from the raging campfire. The curtains looked like they came from the seventies. I was sitting in a rustic log cabin.

121

"Where am I?" I asked.

"You are in Wyoming, the great continental basin," Zandra said, smiling.

"We tracked you here after you disappeared on Saturday. Do you know what happened to you, Ed?" Richard asked.

"Not really. It's hard to explain. After Henderson and Frost left, I helped an old lady get into her van and... Hey, wait a minute. I remember I got stuck with a needle, and everything went blank."

I pulled up my sleeve, and there was a needle mark. Zandra and Richard looked at the mark.

"When I opened my eyes, I was on a Grey spacecraft. We were looking out over the vast high plains and desert as we traveled toward the research center. The Grey who had saved my life was at my side, looking out as we traveled over the area. I know all about the research center. I know its location."

I looked at Zandra, waiting for her response. "I have to help the Grey. He saved my life, Zandra. The Grey needs us to free his pilot and crew before more harm is done to them. The researchers are ruthless and will stop at nothing to achieve their goals. They have already killed one Grey," I said.

"Richard and I have been reassigned, Ed. Chester is back at your apartment, being you until you return. Opus 8 is watching every move you make back there. For now, you are as invisible as you'll ever be," she said.

"Reassigned what do you mean?" I asked.

"We are to find Steve Mann and Tomas Hinter at any cost before Opus 8 does. There are multiple agencies looking for them. So far, no sign of either of them," she replied.

Behind her, there was a knock on the door. It opened slowly. A tall elderly man and an old woman in a wheelchair were in the doorway, looking in at us. The elderly couple entered the cabin and closed the door. I immediately recognized the old woman.

"There you are, young man. I brought Maxwell here to meet you. I see you have visitors," the woman in the wheelchair said, smiling.

She reached up and pulled the wig and rubber mask off. Beneath the makeup and wig was Steve Mann. The elderly man pulled his mask off. It was Tomas Hinter.

"Now that you have found us, I hope you are now free to help us. I promise we both will return with you after we free the Greys," Tomas Hinter said.

Zandra's cell phone rang. "Yes, Violet."

"Zandra, Agents Henderson and Frost are enroute to your location. You have ten minutes before they are at your door."

Zandra put away her cell phone. "Agents Henderson and Frost will be here in less than ten minutes. Ed, head back into the last bedroom. Stay there until I come for you. Steve and Tomas, sit at the table. Act natural when they come in. Keep your hands where they can see them. They might be trigger-happy. Engage them in conversation. We will take care of the rest," she said.

I looked out the window. From the bedroom, I could see the vehicle coming our way. Then I looked back in the hallway where Zandra and Richard had been standing. They were gone.

I heard the SUV pull up. Two doors closed. Moments later, the door swung open. Agent Henderson and Agent Frost entered the cabin, their guns drawn.

"Steve Mann and Tomas Hinter, I presume. We have been looking for you two," Henderson said.

Agent Frost picked up the paper and read the headline out loud. "'Senator Dawson and bodyguard still missing since New Year's Eve. No trace of foul play. The senator's car was found still running on New

123

Year's night on County Road 215. There is a massive multicounty search underway.' I wonder who got the son of a bitch," he said.

"Don't worry about it, Frost. He'll turn up eventually. Probably dead. That happens to people who don't pay their bills. Now that we've found Steve and Tomas, our job will be very simple," Henderson said.

"We aren't hiding, sir. Why are you looking for us? We just decided to take a vacation," Tomas Hinter said convincingly.

"I burned out on the job. It was too demanding, so I decided I wanted to move out west and be a cowboy," Steve Mann said, smiling. "We can't do this here, Frost," Henderson said, putting his gun away.

Suddenly, both he and Frost fell to the ground unconscious. Zandra and Richard had blended in with the coats on the coat rack like two chameleons. Then they shot both men in the neck with blowgun darts, sedating them.

"These guys will be knocked out for a while. Let's put them in the back bedroom. Take their guns, Richard." Zandra looked at the three of us. "We have one chance to do this. We will take Henderson's SUV. I will shape-shift into Henderson. Richard will be Frost's replica. You three will be in the back. When we reach the entrance gate, we will tell the soldiers you three are under arrest. At that time, we will test Violet's new invention. This little round button here produces a vibration wave that knocks a human unconscious. Everyone outside within 150 feet of this device will be affected. That will take out all the outside guards. These special earplugs will protect us when I engage the device. If it works, we get in the easy way," she said.

"What if the invention doesn't work?" I asked.

"It will work, Ed." Richard opened a bag and took five large pistols out. "But if something does go wrong, we have these," he added.

"I thought we never used violence or guns," I said.

"We don't use guns, at least the kind that kills. These are sedating guns. If we need to sedate everyone we meet to get the aliens out alive,

124

we have the firepower. Put the weapon on safety and put it in your coat. After we secure our entry, we all need to put these oxygen masks on to hide our identity. Keep them on at all times," he said. "Tomas, you and Ed will round up the Greys and get them ready for flight. When you get to the building, use this device. Remember, make sure you have those earplugs in." Richard handed me the little button.

"Richard, Steve, and I will secure the hangar. Steve, can you have the hangar ceiling open so the alien craft can exit? We won't have much time," Zandra said.

"Yes, I'll need to activate the sequence code. If they haven't changed it, it will be easy. If they changed it, I'll have to hack into the system. It may take a few minutes," Steve said.

Zandra drove the SUV as Agent Henderson. Richard sat in the other seat; he was Agent Frost. We made our way toward the research center. The drive was long.

"Mr. Pinley, I'm glad you all are helping us. Sorry about sedating you. It was the only way to get you out from under Agents Henderson and Frost safely. As you know, I disappeared over a week ago. When I did, I went to my childhood safe place, my grandparents' slice of paradise. My grandparents are not blood-related. They are my adopted grandparents. No one knows about this. That's the reason Opus 8 or anyone else couldn't find me or Steve." Tomas smiled.

"You were dismissed from the research team," I said.

"I had thoughts of quitting. When they sedated that Grey and tried to do the stage three start-up, I was angered. The watchers saw it and determined that I had to go. Dr. Wilson also filed a complaint. We both were escorted out of the compound and dropped off at our cars. I watched Dr. Wilson drive off. I walked away. I had a feeling that driving a car would not be safe," he said.

We rode in silence for a while. We were all taking in the scenery. Steve looked relieved and happy as we drove toward the research center. When we approached the entry, the guards recognized

Henderson and Frost. One guard approached the window as it rolled down.

"There are three prisoners in the back," Henderson said.

The guard looked in the back seat and gave a thumbs-up. I hit the button on Violet's device, and every guard at the entry collapsed, along with a total of twelve outside guards.

"All right, everyone, put the masks on. Be sure to keep your earplugs in," Zandra said.

*****

Agent Frost opened his eyes. At first, he was unable to focus. The room was dark. He tried to make out the form lying on the bed next to him.

"What the hell happened?" he said as he sat up in his bunk. He looked around. All the blinds were closed; the curtains were drawn. "Henderson, you awake?"

Henderson moved and then slowly sat up. "I've got a sedation hangover, Frost. Try to keep your voice down," he said.

Agent Frost got out of his bunk and slowly made his way into the main room. "Henderson, get in here. You're not going to believe this."

Henderson entered the room. On the bed lay Senator Dawson and Ken Thornton, sleeping.

"Are they alive?" he asked.

"Yes, I saw them move a few seconds ago."

Frost walked into the kitchen. He remembered Henderson and him walking in on Steve Mann and Tomas Hinter. After that, his memory was blank. He felt the back of his neck and felt a welt. "We were ambushed. There must have been someone else here," he said under his breath.

Henderson walked in. "They got our vehicle and our guns. We need to make contact with our people. Frost, I think this whole thing is about the research center. I think Hinter and Mann are going to try to release the captive Greys, and God knows what else," he said. "I'll make the call, Frost. Get the senator and his sidekick ready to travel."

Frost walked into the back bedroom. "Senator Dawson, wake up." He looked at the clock. It was 3:33 p.m. He recalled arriving at 5:23 a.m. Shortly after that, they had been sedated.

Senator Dawson opened his eyes and looked at Agent Frost. "Senator, can you hear me?"

The senator just stared at Frost, wide-eyed. "Senator Dawson, do you know where you are?"

"In my car. The lights are so bright. I'm in my car. I'm looking for Ken. He's gone. So is the bag that body is in. It's gone." Senator Dawson screamed out and then closed his eyes. A few seconds later, he opened his eyes again. He looked around the room. "Where's Ken?"

"Ken is over in the next bunk," Agent Frost said as he tried to wake Ken up.

When Ken finally opened his eyes, he didn't speak. He just stared forward.

"Ken, do you hear me?" Senator Dawson said.

There was no reaction from Ken. Agent Frost waited.

"Where did they take you, Ken? Why did they take you and not me? Answer me, Ken. After the lights came, what happened?"

Ken looked around the room. Then he spoke. "I don't know, Senator. I don't remember anything. I saw the lights, and that was it for me. I don't recall anything. What time is it? Where are we?"

"The time is 3:56 p.m., February 2, and you are somewhere in Wyoming," Agent Frost said.

"But it was New Year's Eve when we met you," the senator said. "That's right. They found your car running on the side of the road. No sign of either of you. And now you show up here in some cabin in the middle of nowhere, along with me and my partner," Agent Frost said.

Agent Henderson finished his phone call and entered the room. "How did you both get here?" Ken asked, half engaged.

"We came to arrest two people we thought might be renting this cabin. When we arrived, we were ambushed, sedated, and left back in the bedroom. When we regained consciousness, we discovered you both here," Agent Henderson said.

"What do you remember, Ken?" Senator Dawson asked. "Nothing. I saw the lights, and that's it. Now a month later, I'm here. I don't remember anything," Ken said.

"I don't remember anything either. I thought that I was left and that they took Ken. I panicked, then everything went dark. I think the aliens took the alien body and the two of us. They probably were the ones who ambushed the two of you," the senator said.

"We know who ambushed us, Senator. I'm sure it wasn't the aliens. Frost, call Major Samuels. He will need our location. Let him know they will be picking up the four of us," Agent Henderson said. Ken Thornton sat up. "We need to get our story right, Senator.

This could be the end of the line for all of us," he said. He seemed to be a lot sharper and now awake.

"What do you mean 'all of us'? Frost and I don't have anything to do with you two," Henderson said.

"Wait, Henderson, what are we going tell them? You both are as chin-deep in shit as we are. We can't let them know about our deal. The money and the alien body need to be kept a secret," Ken said.

"What money? We never got any money. As for the body bag with the dead alien in it, we never saw it, Senator. So you better have your ducks in a row. You will need to recall your alien abduction during your

128

debriefing. It's up to you whether you want to disclose the body bag with the dead alien in it. After all, you guys are the only ones who know about it. If I were you, I wouldn't say anything about the body bag. You have enough to explain, all the missing time and the big question: why were you guys out there on County Road 215 on New Year's Eve?" Henderson asked.

Frost followed Agent Henderson while calling Major Samuels on his cell phone. A few minutes later, Frost put his cell phone down. "Samuels said the power and the security cameras went offline twenty minutes ago at the research center. They cannot reach anyone there by phone, so they have already called out the cavalry. The gunships should arrive in thirty-five minutes. They expect to have us picked up in ten minutes," he said.

*****

We all got out of the SUV. Zandra, Steve, and Richard headed toward the hangar. Tomas and I headed for the area where the Greys were being held.

We approached the door and waited outside. Tomas pushed the button and waited, then he slipped the entry card in. We slowly opened the door. I could see that the research staff were all lying on the floor unconscious. Some of them were at their desks. I couldn't see any guards.

We walked in and saw that there was another locked door requiring a card key one we didn't have. Tomas looked around and found a research assistant with the entry card. He opened the metal door.

Down the hall was another metal door with a screened safety window. Inside, we could see the Greys. "They look tired," Tomas said. "We need to get their suits for flight. They are probably in this equipment room."

He opened the door, and we gathered twelve suits. He then opened the metal door. He stood there, looking at the Greys. I think he was communicating with them.

He looked at me. "They are ready. Let's hand out the suits," he said.

We got everyone suited up and headed for the hangar. It was a short walk. We approached the hangar slowly. Tomas opened the door with the card key and looked inside. The guards and research staff were all unconscious. The Greys walked in and waited.

Tomas and Steve began working on the Grey spacecraft, unlocking the chains and holding devices to allow the spacecraft to ascend when ready. Steve opened the craft's door. Inside, the lights and control panels lit up. The Greys entered the spacecraft and took their seats. The pilot sat behind the control panel. He placed his hand on the glass panel. A blue light glowed around his hand, and the spacecraft began to vibrate and glow. Zandra and Richard watched as the craft began to levitate.

"All right, let's open the ceiling." Steve Mann walked over to a large control panel and pushed a red button. The ceiling began to open just like the aperture on a camera.

From somewhere behind the research desks, a series of automatic weapons were suddenly fired. Steve fell backward with two blood-soaked holes in his chest. He sat on the ground, blood spreading all around him. There was another spray of gunshots that ricocheted off the spacecraft. Tomas and I crawled along the floor. I had dropped my button somewhere, and I was looking for it.

I heard a concussion bomb go off, knocking everyone at the entrance to the ground. I saw my button; it was about fifteen feet in front of me. I started to crawl toward it, when I saw a guard run over and grab the button, his weapon pointed at Tomas. He opened fire just as he pushed the button. He collapsed, his finger on the trigger, emptying his gun. Tomas lay unconscious. He had been hit, but I couldn't tell how badly. Zandra and Richard were attending to Steve Mann.

"The ceiling is open. They just need to go now," Tomas moaned.

Zandra had managed to stop Steve's bleeding. Both men were in bad shape. We needed to transport them out. Richard had Violet on his cell phone. He was giving her our coordinates for the portal to open. It was our only escape now. In the distance, we could hear the military gunships heading our way.

"We need to get out into the yard. Violet will activate the portal there," Richard said.

We picked Tomas and Steve up and carried them outside, to the center of the large yard.

"This is it. All we can do now is wait for the portal to activate. When it does, we step into it, and we are gone," Zandra said as she knelt next to Steve. He was having trouble breathing. Richard was tending to Tomas, trying to control his bleeding. Ahead of us, four gunships hovered fifty feet off the ground, coming at us, their guns aimed and ready. They were maybe fifty feet from us.

"Richard, I can't find your location! The portal won't activate!" Violet's voice boomed from Richard's cell phone.

"Keep trying, Violet. Goodbye." Richard put his phone down. "I guess this is it, Zandra. It's been a long run."

He reached out and grabbed Zandra's hand. She smiled and looked at him. She reached over and took my hand. Tomas and Steve lay dying on the ground next to us. We watched as the gunships opened their guns on us. I could see the flash of the machine-guns, their barrels red-hot. I closed my eyes and waited for the impact.

Nothing happened.

I opened my eyes. We were all standing on the viewing deck of a Grey spacecraft. Tomas and Steve were being cared for by the Greys. They rushed them away to surgery in hopes of saving their lives.

We watched from the viewing deck, thousands of feet above the research center's yard. The gunships were firing on everything in the outside area. They took out all the outbuildings. They destroyed Henderson's vehicle, which was parked inside the research center's parking area. Then the ropes came out, and the assault team descended onto the ground. Their guns were ready as they searched the area for us. It was clear they were not going to take any survivors.

"That is why it was so important that Opus 8 did not gain knowledge of our advanced technology."

I heard the voice of the Grey inside my head. I felt a little ashamed and uncomfortable.

"Mr. Pinley, I do not want to make you feel uncomfortable. I also must be honest with everyone," the Grey's voice said inside my head.

We watched as the assault team searched for five suspects last seen in the very courtyard they had just demolished. Nothing could have escaped that barrage of weaponry, machine-guns firing away. They were not going to take prisoners, and they didn't. No one was found, alive or dead. There was just blood pooled up on the asphalt where Steve and Tomas had lain. In the distance, we could see the parade of government vehicles coming up to the entrance of the research center. The viewing screen closed.

"We are grateful for your help. Two hours ago, the United States withdrew from Opus 8, along with other Western European countries. The US Air Force is in pursuit of those gunships now. When they catch them, they will force them to land at Fort Smith. This is the beginning of a transformation between humans and our kind. Our road will be long and difficult, but achievable," the Grey said.

The Grey left the room, and three chairs appeared from out of the wall. Richard, Zandra, and I sat down. I lay my head back and relaxed.

I must have closed my eyes and fallen asleep. When I awoke, I was in my apartment, on my couch. I could hear Chester making coffee in the kitchen. The coffee grinder screamed out while Chester sang whatever opera was on his mind, a torturous blend of harmonious rhythms. I was home. It felt great.

About the Author

E*d Pinley: Paranormal Investigator* is Lester Roger's debut novel. Lester spent nine years as a DJ at KDNK community public radio Carbondale Colorado; his show featured comedy written by him as well as featuring touring bands and performers live in the studio. He is also a singer and songwriter, and he plays with the band Stone Kitchen.

Lester's life adventures started out in Northern Wisconsin as a teenager, hitchhiking across the country and jumping freight trains west. Traveling the country provided the stimulus for his imagination to consider what some may think are wild ideas, such as other possible life forms in the universe, parallel dimensions, and the possibility of portals or wormholes opening up to other worlds. He currently resides in Western Colorado.

Made in the USA
Monee, IL
04 August 2024